Heartland

Beyond the Horizon

Heartland

❧

Share every moment. . . .

Coming Home

After the Storm

Breaking Free

Taking Chances

Come What May

One Day You'll Know

Out of the Darkness

Thicker Than Water

Every New Day

Tomorrow's Promise

True Enough

Sooner or Later

Darkest Hour

Everything Changes

Love Is a Gift

Holding Fast

A Season of Hope

New Beginnings

From This Day On

Always There

Heartland

❧

Beyond the Horizon

by Lauren Brooke

SCHOLASTIC INC.

New York Toronto London Auckland Sydney
Mexico City New Delhi Hong Kong Buenos Aires

ISBN 10: 0-439-91610-0
ISBN 13: 978-0-439-91610-3

Heartland series created by Working Partners Ltd., London.

Copyright © 2007 by Working Partners Ltd.
Published by Scholastic Inc. All rights reserved.

SCHOLASTIC and associated logos are trademarks and/or registered trademarks of Scholastic Inc. HEARTLAND is a trademark and/or registered trademark of Working Partners Ltd.

12 11 10 9 8 7 6 5 4 3 2 1   7 8 9 10 11 12/0
Printed in the U.S.A.   40
First printing, April 2007

With special thanks to
Elisabeth Faith

Chapter One

"Has someone taken Jupiter's stable bandages? I swear I left them on the shelf in the tack room."

Noting the stressed tone of her friend's voice, Amy stopped grooming Ashia, a striking dapple gray quarter horse, and looked over the partition wall. Although the air was frosty enough to make her breath come out in clouds, her enthusiasm and effort to clean up Ashia had made her hot, and she was happy to have a reason to pause for a moment.

Katie, one of her classmates in the pre-veterinary program at Virginia Tech, was walking down the center aisle of the barn. She raised her hands in a helpless gesture. "I've got a zillion things to do to get ready to go home for spring break," she told Amy, "but I have to

1

find Jupe's bandages first. It's probably a sign that I'm not supposed to go to San Francisco. Maybe something disastrous is going to happen over the vacation."

"I'll help you look," Amy offered. Katie was great fun, but tended to indulge in melodrama whenever the chance arose. Sometimes Amy thought she would have been better suited for studying drama like her best friend, Soraya. Amy and Soraya had been e-mailing and talking on the phone throughout their first year away from home, especially during the rather wobbly period when Soraya had split up with her boyfriend, Matt. Even though the split had been amicable, some intense phone support had been required from Amy during the weekend that Soraya broke things off. She was now going out with a new guy, Anthony; Amy hadn't met him yet but it sounded like Soraya was totally head over heels.

Thinking of Soraya reminded Amy of how excited she was to be headed back to Heartland for spring break. Along with being home and seeing her family, Amy knew she and Soraya were due for some quality girl-time.

Amy slipped out of Ashia's stall and bolted the door securely behind her. Although the mare was unlikely to attempt escaping with her strained tendon injury, Amy wasn't taking any chances.

Virginia Tech treated a variety of animals as part of the students' practical studies but, of course, the equine unit was what Amy enjoyed most. The students were all assigned different animals to look after each week and Amy had been involved in the X-raying and diagnosis of Ashia's tendon injury. The beautiful gray wouldn't ever be able to return to the rigors of three-day eventing but, if her injury was allowed time to heal properly, she would still be able to be used as a hack and perhaps even jump at the local level shows.

"Oh, I guess Sharona found them," Katie said, looking at a tall girl walking toward them waving the bandages. "Thanks anyway, Amy."

"For some reason, they were in my grooming kit," Sharona explained, handing them over.

"How did they get there?" Katie wondered. "Whatever. It's lucky you found them. I can go start packing as soon as I've got these on Jupe."

"Does that mean you've decided to risk going to San Francisco after all?" Amy grinned.

"A girl's got to live on the edge once in a while," Katie replied with a playful smirk as she opened the stall across the aisle. Jupiter, a seventeen-hand chestnut gelding who was being treated for a skin complaint, flashed his ears back nervously. He was a high-strung event horse and was nervous of his new surroundings. Amy's fingers itched to use T-touch on him to help soothe away his fear. She always used the massage method to help settle anxious animals back at Heartland, where horses who were physically injured or emotionally distressed were

sent to be rehabilitated. Even if being at the veterinary
college wasn't like being back home where Amy could
pick and choose which horse to care for, at least she was
allowed to use T-touch on the horses she was assigned.
Her professors had been really interested in the alternative methods she had grown up with; she would never
forget the thrill of being asked to speak about the work
they did at Heartland at a local boarding school during
her first term. She'd given the lecture at Chestnut Hill
and the positive response from the young students had
been thrilling.

"Wild horses couldn't keep Sharona from leaving
tomorrow," Leila called from the stall alongside Ashia.
The dark-haired student balanced her grooming kit on
the half wall and winked at Amy. "The IPC needs her
too much!"

Amy hid a grin. For the last two weeks, Sharona had
been telling anyone who would listen that she was doing
her work experience at the International Polo Club in
Palm Beach. Everyone was genuinely glad that Sharona's
dad, who knew the chief veterinarian there, had managed to set up the internship. But there was a limit to the
number of times any of them could listen to Sharona
brag about how she was going to spend her week surrounded by A-list show horses and hot Argentinean
polo players. *Not everyone gets to have such a glamorous*

opportunity, Amy thought as she returned to Ashia's stall. Not that she would want to be anywhere other than Heartland for spring break. She missed being part of the daily routine and of so many different horses' journeys to recovery. She had arranged to do her work experience with her brother-in-law, Scott. He was going to take her on his morning rounds each day and Amy was really looking forward to putting her college learning into practice at his veterinary clinic.

"Speaking of the IPC, did I tell you guys that Adolfo Cambiaso has offered to give me a polo lesson?" Sharona threw the question out to anyone who was in the vicinity.

"Only about a hundred times, but it's always worth one more announcement," a male voice teased.

Amy smiled as Will Savage led Spider into a nearby stall. It was Will's turn to bring him up from the paddocks. One of their lecturer's kept the blue roan at the college during the school year. With the new grass sprouting, the horses were only allowed out for part of each day to avoid getting colic or laminitis.

"Oh, I'm rolling on the floor with laughter. You're sooo funny, Will," Sharona shot back. She left Jupiter's stall and walked over to look in at Amy. "Are you still going home for spring break, Amy?"

"Yes." She tried not to sound defensive; she had already

overheard Sharona telling Katie that she thought Amy was getting out of doing any real work by going home.

"Aren't you worried that you won't learn as much by working on your home turf?" Sharona's blue eyes looked full of concern, but Amy got the feeling the look wasn't really genuine.

"Well, going home certainly won't get me any credit for glamour, but if hard work and working alongside an experienced, professional vet counts for anything then I think I'll do just fine." Amy smiled to take any sting out of her words. "I appreciate your concern, though."

"It sounds to me as if Sharona's going to be too busy with the players to worry about earning credits," Will called from the adjacent stall in a stage whisper. "Do you think we should e-mail the club and remind them that she is there to learn, not to work on her tan and master the finer aspects of polo?"

Amy stifled a giggle as Sharona scowled in Will's direction. "Well, I'd rather be spending my spare time learning how to play polo than hanging around with a herd of wild steers." She tossed her braided black hair off her shoulder. "Anyway, I've got to go finish my packing."

"Later," Amy said before turning her attention back to Will. "Speaking of wild steers, are you all ready for Arizona?" she asked as she took Ashia's bandages out of the cold water they'd been soaking in. She squeezed them until they were nearly dry and then bent down to put the first one on.

"As ready as I can be. It sounds like I'm in for a real adventure," Will told Amy with enthusiasm. "Do you want a hand with that?"

Amy glanced up to see that he had left Spider's stall and was standing by Ashia's door watching her bandage the horse. "That would be great, thanks," she nodded.

She noticed that before Will joined her, he offered Ashia his hand to smell and then rubbed her nose. He didn't have a huge amount of experience around horses, but from what she had seen, his instincts were amazing. Will waited until Ashia's ears were forward before he moved to crouch down by Amy.

"It's so great that you were able to get a place on a ranch," she said as she finished wrapping the first of the bandages around Ashia's hindleg. "It seems like you're so perfect for it."

"Yeah, I can't wait. I was starting to worry it was going to fall through but they finally called a few days ago to confirm that I could go. Nothing like leaving it to the last minute." He grinned, his midnight blue eyes twinkling.

Amy had to smile in return. Will was one of the most popular students in her program with his laid-back attitude and easy humor — his good looks didn't hurt, either. But she knew better than to underestimate his talent with animals or academics. When they'd teamed up to work on a research project on feline leukemia, Amy had found it hard to keep up with how hard he worked.

"Here." She handed him a bandage. "Can you do her other hind leg?"

"You might want to give me a quick demo," Will replied. "We wouldn't want to come back to the stall and find I've put it on so loose that Ash shook the thing off."

Amy chuckled. "The trick is to make sure it's taut but not too restrictive," she told him, gently wrapping the bandage over Ashia's tendon. "And make sure it's looser here than on the leg bone."

"I think I can manage that," Will said, taking a bandage and moving to Ashia's foreleg. His curly dark red hair fell charmingly into his eyes as he leaned forward and began to wrap the bandage.

"I was a little surprised that you decided to do your internship with cows and horses," Amy teased. "I thought dogs were more your thing." Will's knowledge of dogs was incredible. He liked to joke about a time when he had performed an emergency tracheotomy on his pet dog, Rufus, after a bone had gotten stuck in his throat. Amy had never met anyone who could tease as convincingly as Will and for a few moments she had almost believed him. He never could hide the mischief in his eyes, though, and she'd soon detected the playful sparkle.

"I figure I should get more experience with horses," Will explained earnestly. "I took a couple of trail-riding vacations with my parents when I was younger that were fantastic, but I'd like to get to a point where I can really get into it on my own."

Amy suspected that he was underplaying his skills. Will seemed like the kind of guy who was good at everything he tried. And it wasn't just animals he was great with. He'd confessed to Amy when they were doing their research project that he'd turned down a soccer scholarship at the University of Virginia to come to Virginia Tech.

"So I guess you must be psyched about going home and seeing your family," Will commented as he stood back from Ashia's bandaged leg.

"Yeah, I can't wait to see everyone again. My sister's going to have her baby in a couple of months, and she was barely showing the last time I was home. I can't believe how soon I'm going to be an aunt!" Amy exclaimed.

"Your boyfriend must be looking forward to you coming back, too." Will continued as he walked around Ashia to put on the final bandage.

Amy hesitated, feeling awkward. Will had asked her to be his date at a party just before Christmas break, and she'd told him about Ty when she'd gently turned him down. "We're *both* looking forward to seeing each other," she said truthfully.

"How's he handling you being away?" Will asked without taking his eyes off of Ashia.

"Oh, he's a typical guy and doesn't talk too much about his feelings." She made her reply light-hearted. Amy didn't mention how excited she was to spend a whole week back at Heartland with Ty — the distance had been tough on both of them and she couldn't wait for them to reconnect. But for some reason she just didn't want to talk with Will about her relationship. "Do you think you could finish up on your own? I thought I'd go start giving out the evening feeds."

"No problem," Will told her. "I'll come give you a hand as soon as I'm done."

Amy let herself out of the stall and headed down to the storeroom. All of the horses seemed to know why she'd come, judging by the way they were looking over their doors with pricked ears. As Amy walked past Sunlight, the palomino kicked his door.

"It's coming, boy," Amy promised. She paused to scratch his temple. The gelding had been brought in by his owner the day before because he had started to have fits. But he was the picture of health at the moment as he waited for his evening meal.

As Amy's fingers worked softly against the palomino's skin, her thoughts returned to Ty. *He and Joni are probably busy mucking out the stalls and getting the evening feeds ready, too.* She pictured her boyfriend pushing a wheelbarrow across the yard, his dark hair falling over his forehead, his green eyes narrowed against the sun. *I can't wait to be with him again.* As much as she loved being at college, she'd been disappointed at how little time either of them had had to talk on the phone or e-mail. From the moment she woke until the moment she finally got to bed, she was engrossed in exams, lectures, and assignments. *But at least we'll have my break together,* Amy thought as she gave Sunlight a final pat.

Amy set out two lines of four buckets each and shook a packet of white powder into Oliver's, which was clearly labeled. All of the buckets had horses' names on them so that if any medication needed to be put into the feed it wouldn't go to the wrong animal. "Now for some cod liver oil," Amy mused aloud as she reached up to the supplement shelf and took down the large drum.

She finished filling the feed buckets, concentrating on making sure the correct amount of each supplement was put out.

"Are you done?" Will teased from the doorway. "Since you already cracked the whip and had me bandage Ashia, don't try to tell me you need me to do all the feeds.

I'm going to be worn out by the time you're through with me."

"I doubt that," Amy said with a laugh. "But I'll try my best. There are eight hay nets that need to be put out."

Will gave an exaggerated sigh. "A man's work is never done."

"That's right. So you might as well check the water buckets while you're at it," Amy snapped, trying to sound mean but barely suppressing a smile.

"I'll learn to keep my mouth shut next time," Will pretended to complain.

"You? Never!" Amy shot back, and then burst into laughter.

As Amy picked up the feed buckets she was reminded of the banter back at Heartland among herself, Ty, and Joni. Suddenly, a wave of homesickness washed over her that she hadn't experienced since the first month of college. She couldn't wait to get back.

"Don't worry, Oliver, there's nothing weird in it," she reassured the bay gelding as he blew suspiciously at his feed. *Nothing you're going to taste, anyway,* she thought, crossing her fingers. Oliver had refused to take his morning feed with antibiotic powder in it so this time Amy had poured some apple juice in to mask the taste. With one last sniff, Oliver took a tentative mouthful. "Good boy," Amy said, and gave his shoulder a pat. "How's that leg doing?" Oliver's foreleg had puffed up like a balloon because of an infection. He lived outdoors and his owner didn't have a stable, so Oliver had come to the veterinary college in order to have some shelter while the infection was clearing up.

She gently probed the inflamed skin and was pleased to feel that the heat had disappeared. Oliver's leg felt cool to the touch, a sure sign the infection was clearing.

"Knock, knock," Will said, letting himself into the stall. He took the sweet-smelling hay net over to the ring in the wall and tied it securely. "I swear these horses are fed better than we are."

"Don't let Emily hear you say that," Amy replied. Emily managed the cash register in the cafeteria at lunchtime and always commented on how good everyone's food looked. Once or twice she'd even asked Amy if she could taste what she had on her tray to help her decide what to eat when she got off work.

"She'd probably want to arrange a tasting session," Will said with a grin. "I had to swat her fingers off my lasagna yesterday."

Amy laughed, picturing the scene.

She finished giving out the other feed buckets, and then helped Will with the last of the hay nets.

Amy took a wide, flat broom and swept the center aisle while the horses ate, and Will went to clean up the feed room. It didn't take long to gather and wash out the buckets once the horses were finished eating. Amy neatly stacked them and then headed out of the barn with Will.

They walked in silence through the yard and past the cat and dog kennels to the main path that led to the heart of the campus. Amy looked up at the blocks of red brick buildings with their windows glinting in the evening sunlight and found it hard to believe that she had been here for almost two semesters. She still got a thrill from attending lectures in the huge auditoriums and keeping up with the frantic schedule of her first year. It was tiring and there were times when she wished she never had to write another essay again, but there was no denying how awesome the last few months had been. She'd barely had time for the homesickness she'd felt when she had first left Heartland and Ty. But it was so good to think that tomorrow she'd be heading home.

"Just think, in twenty-four hours you'll be in Arizona," Amy said as they walked toward the student residences.

"Hanging out with wild steer," Will replied, mimicking Sharona before breaking into a wide smile. "I've always wanted to ride in a western-style saddle. It looks like sitting in a big armchair."

"Yeah, well, that armchair still has a horse with four moving legs and a mind of its own underneath it," Amy warned. "So, do you have any idea what kind of veterinary work you'll be doing?"

"It will mainly be large animal — obviously, with the cattle and horses on the ranch — but I'll also be going out with the local vet on some of his calls," Will told her. "There's going to be a cattle drive at the end of the week so there are supposed to be a lot of people there to help out. My friend went last year and said he had a fantastic time."

"What happens during a cattle drive?" Amy asked with interest.

"Basically, you ride out on horses to the land where the cows spent the winter and round them all up. Then you bring the herd back to the ranch, brand any new calves, and make sure the herd is healthy. After that, you drive them out again and leave them where they'll graze for the summer." Will seemed to glow as he talked about it. "Usually you spend at least one night camping. The whole thing sounds incredible."

"It really does," Amy said, envying Will for one brief moment.

"You could always give them a call and see if there's a space for you, too," Will suggested.

As much as Amy would have loved to experience life on a working ranch, she knew it couldn't tempt her away from going home. She wanted to gallop Sundance over Clairdale Ridge and see for herself how three-year-old Spindle was responding to being lunged fully tacked up. She would never miss visiting with Lou now that she was in her last couple of months of the pregnancy or enjoying mornings with Grandpa. And she wanted to feel Ty's arms around her once again. She shook her head. "Thanks, Will, but I'm happy to be going home."

Home. The word sang in her heart as they turned off the main path and walked up the steps that led to the quad. *I'm going home — home to Heartland.*

Chapter Two

That night, Amy crammed her college textbooks into her backpack and wondered when she'd find time to do any reading when she had so much work to do between helping out at Heartland and her internship with Scott. She brushed her finger over a picture she had on her desk of Ty sitting on the paddock gate with Spindle nosing at his pocket for a treat. *This time tomorrow I'll be with them!*

"Hey Aim, we're going to the coffee shop. Wanna come?" Amy's roommate, India, asked as she walked into the room. Amy gave India a smile as she moved over to her fully packed suitcase and began to hunt through the layers of clothes. She found the suede jacket she was looking for and shook out the folds.

"That sounds perfect." Amy buckled her backpack and put it on her desk. She was all ready to leave first thing in the morning and grabbing coffee with her friends would be a good chance to say good-bye.

"Cool." India fluffed out her hair and peered into the full-length mirror inside her closet door.

"You look great." Amy smiled. Professor Macintosh, their animal husbandry professor, often said that if India paid as much attention in her classes as she did to her appearance, she'd be a straight-A student.

India pushed back her hair so it tumbled over her shoulders in a cascade of red curls. "Thanks. Do you think this is too casual?" she asked, gesturing to her black pants and V-neck sweater.

"It's just coffee," Amy said with a laugh, pressing her hand into India's back and pushing her out of the room. "You don't get an extra espresso shot for being a fashion icon!"

"I swear I must have accidentally checked a box on my housing form, requesting a roomie who'd keep me grounded," India pretended to grumble.

Amy linked arms with her roommate as they headed down to their favorite café. It suddenly hit her that as much as she couldn't wait to get home, she might actually miss her new friends while she was away.

❧

Amy ran up to the bus terminal on campus. It was two minutes to seven but she couldn't help worrying that the bus had come early. Coffee the night before had turned into a late-night game of Trivial Pursuit, and Amy hadn't even heard her first alarm go off. *Thank goodness I set two or I'd still be in bed!* She breathed a sigh of relief as the bus rumbled toward her, right on time. She would transfer at the main station downtown where she could catch another bus straight through to her hometown in the north of the state.

Amy shouldered her bag while the bus pulled up. After boarding, she headed toward a seat in the back. She stowed her bag on the luggage rack and as she sat down she could see someone waving through the window. She shifted to look more closely and saw that it was Will. *Is he catching the same bus?* Amy wondered, pleased at the thought of sharing the journey with him. But then she noticed that he didn't have any luggage.

"Have a great break," Will mouthed through the glass.

Amy smiled and waved back. It was so nice of Will to see her off.

She thought back to the last time she'd traveled home for Christmas break. Ty had been waiting for her at the bus stop. He'd taken her backpack and swung it over his shoulder before wrapping his arms around her and holding her very close. Amy leaned back in her seat and enjoyed the luxury of thinking about her boyfriend. *Maybe Ty and I can go out tomorrow night to catch a movie. It will be so amazing to have some time just to ourselves.* Amy smiled to herself. Suddenly, the time she had at home didn't seem like it could possibly be long enough!

❦

During the last leg of her journey home, Amy found herself struggling to keep her eyes open. She had read the open page of her textbook three times and the words still didn't make any sense. When the bus pulled up at the terminal, she was relieved to be able to put the book away.

Lou had arranged to meet her because Ty was busy in the stables. Amy jumped off the bus and scanned the parking lot for her sister's car. She couldn't see it anywhere, which was odd because the bus had been ten minutes late getting in. Amy felt the stirrings of worry for her sister. *What if the baby is early?* With her heart racing, she pulled her cell phone out of her pocket and saw that it was turned off.

Amy turned on the phone, dialed her sister's number, and hit SEND. Her sister answered it on the second ring.

"Lou, thank goodness. I thought something was wrong!" Amy said as soon as she heard her sister's voice.

"I've been trying to get through to you for the last half an hour but it kept going straight to voicemail," Lou told her.

"I forgot I turned it off last night," Amy explained. "Are you OK? Where are you?"

"That's why I've been calling," Lou replied. "I'm still at home. Well," she corrected herself, "at Heartland. My ankles puffed up and I need to keep them elevated. Could you get a cab? I'm so sorry there's no one else to come out to meet you. Ty still hasn't come back from returning a horse to its owner, and Grandpa's out with Nancy."

"That's OK," Amy said. "It's no problem getting a cab. I'll see if I can pick up a treat for you from the bakery in town."

"You're an angel." Lou sounded tired. "I should say no, but it's not like I can get any fatter," she added with a chuckle.

Amy smiled. "I'll see you in about twenty minutes," she promised.

As she headed into town she wondered if she'd have time to work with Spindle that afternoon. One of the first things she'd do when she got home was go see him and Sundance. She quickened her speed along the sidewalk, feeling a fresh surge of longing to get back home. She could almost hear the horses whinnying in welcome!

❧

Amy leaned out of the cab window as the car drove up the long road to Heartland. She took in a deep breath of air as she waited for her first glimpse of the house. *There!* The familiar white-painted clapboards gleamed through a break in the trees. She scanned the paddocks but they were empty. Someone must have already brought the horses in for the evening.

The cab pulled up outside the main house and Amy paid the driver and jumped out. She noticed that the Heartland trailer was in its usual place, which meant that Ty was back from his drop-off. She glanced over at the barn that stood a short distance from the main house. She would love to go over to see Ty and the horses, but she knew she wouldn't be able to tear herself away quickly, and Lou was expecting her.

"Hello," she called, kicking off her boots at the kitchen door. "It's me!"

There was no answer and the house felt empty as Amy crossed the kitchen floor and went into the living room. Her sister was lying on the sofa with a patchwork blanket over her. The magazine she'd been reading had fallen out of her hand to cover her bulging stomach and she was fast asleep.

Lou's eyelids flickered as Amy sat down on the edge of the sofa. As Amy took her sister's hand, she was struck by how tired Lou looked. She'd mentioned in one of their weekly conversations that her energy level was zilch lately but Amy hadn't really understood why she would be so worn out, until she saw how pregnant her sister was. Now it was starting to make sense. She'd be wiped out too if she had to carry another person around in her belly all day!

"Hello, stranger." Lou yawned before smiling up at her. "It's so good to see you."

Amy leaned down to hug her sister. "It's great to be seen."

"I'm so sorry I couldn't come get you. I meant to at least have something to drink ready for when you walked in, and what happened? I fell asleep. It's not much of a homecoming welcome."

"I'd rather you just relax," Amy said, gently laying her hand on Lou's tummy. She felt a hard kick as if her future niece was objecting to the pressure. "Wow! You didn't mention you had a martial arts expert in there."

"Tell me about it. This kid is going to be *some* kind of athlete, for sure." Lou gave a rueful smile as Amy tucked the blanket in around her. "Do you recognize it?" she asked, brushing her hand over the multicolored patchwork squares.

Amy frowned. "I don't think so."

"Our grandmother made it for Mom when she was expecting me. She used to wrap you in it when you were a baby, too. I found it in a box in the attic a few months ago when I was taking all of my things over to the new house."

"And now your daughter will be tucked up in it," Amy

said. *I bet when Mom wrapped this around Lou she never dreamed she'd not be around to do the same for her grand-daughter.* Amy's eyes began to sting with tears. She jumped up. "Listen, I'll go make us some tea and cut us a slice of the cake I got in town."

"Herbal for me, please." Lou yawned again. "The tea bags are in the container next to the coffee jar."

Amy went into the kitchen to make the drinks. She glanced at the clock on the wall. Usually, at this time she'd be running to a class with some of her friends. It was hard to shake off the feeling that right now she should be frantically scribbling notes, trying to keep up with Professor Macintosh's infamously detailed lectures.

She poured hot water into mugs over tea bags, cut the cake into slices, and then carried it all into the living room. Lou's breathing was deep and regular, and Amy wasn't surprised to find that her sister had fallen asleep again. Deciding against waking her, she put the tray down on the table just in case Lou woke up soon, then tiptoed from the room and made a beeline for the barn.

The moment Amy walked through the large double doors she knew she was really home. The familiar smell of fresh hay, the rattle of buckets, and the occasional contented snort made Amy stop for a moment. She tipped back her head and inhaled deeply.

"Excuse me, miss, can I help you?" Ty's voice, tinged with amusement, came from behind her.

Amy spun around to see Ty with a bale of hay on his shoulder. He dropped it to the ground as she raced to throw her arms around him. "I missed you!"

Ty laughed. "And here I was thinking that you didn't have the time."

Amy felt a quick stab of guilt. It was true that at college she had to be one hundred percent focused on her classes to get good grades, but she hated the thought that Ty would take her unavailability personally. "Here, hold still, you've got more hay in your hair than in the bale." She brushed out the strands of hay with her hand.

"You've changed your perfume," Ty said when Amy was done.

"Do you like it?" she asked. "A bunch of us went shopping last weekend and we stopped by a perfume counter. I thought it was time to try something new."

She wanted to bite the words back as soon as they were out of her mouth. Ty had given her perfume a year ago and, until recently, she hadn't worn anything else since.

Ty's expression stayed neutral so Amy couldn't tell if he was hurt or not. "Are there any other changes I should know about?"

"Nope, otherwise it's just regular old me." She smiled.

"Well, in that case, I'd better give you a tour of the horses and bring you up to speed," Ty replied. He picked up the bale of hay and leaned it against the nearby wall.

"We haven't had any new arrivals in the last week, which makes Tarren the most recent." He led Amy over to the first stall. "Do you remember me mentioning that she came to us around this time last week?"

Amy remembered Ty describing Tarren on the phone last week. Her bridle had broken while riding cross-country and both the mare and the rider had taken a nasty fall at the water jump. "This is the horse who's lost her nerve and won't go near water, right?" She knew that Tarren's owner was eager to start riding the competition circuit as soon as her broken ribs were healed, but her horse needed to be persuaded to put her trust in her rider again.

She whistled softly to the bay mare who was eating her feed. Tarren looked up and stared at Amy before dropping her head back to her bucket.

"I love the white star on her forehead," Amy commented, admiring the mare. Even though Tarren stood at sixteen hands high, she had a small, neat-shaped head that made her seem more petite than she really was.

"Yep, not that it's brought her much luck," Ty replied as he leaned his elbows on the door. "But I managed to get her to stand still while I ran the hose over her hooves today. I'd say she's on the road to recovery."

"That's great!" Amy said enthusiastically. The British-bred sport horse oozed quality with her part-Irish draught, part-Thoroughbred breeding. She deserved to be flying around a cross-country course with all of the quiet calm that was written in her wide-set eyes.

"Why are we so empty?" Amy asked as Ty walked with her to the opposite stall. From what she could tell, the barn was only half full.

"I had to cut back with Joni being away. I knew that you were coming home but you won't be able to take on a lot of work in the yard in addition to your work with Scott." Amy gave Ty a questioning look and he held his hands up defensively. "I had to make a judgment call about how much work I knew we could get through."

Amy tried to push away the feeling of irritation that Ty hadn't checked with her first. When she'd been living at home and going to school she'd managed to still help out in the stables. Why did Ty think she wouldn't be able to do that now?

Not wanting to start an argument, she looked over the door at a strikingly marked horse. "You must be Heart's Ease, you handsome fellow," she murmured.

She held out her hand to the Appaloosa gelding, who pricked his ears forward in return. He'd arrived at Heartland a couple of days before Tarren. Ty had phoned to tell her that the gelding's appetite had been declining. "Has he been eating?"

"Not as much as he should be," Ty replied. "It's barely enough to keep a Shetland going. Joni's being amazing, though. She's come up with about a hundred different recipes to tempt him!"

"What kinds of food are you trying?" Amy reached out her hand to scratch Heart's Ease's nose as he came to the door.

"Well, in addition to different food combinations, we're giving him Fenugreek to stimulate his appetite. The problem is, he eats the new food once or twice and then loses interest in it. Joni says that if he's no better by the time she gets back, she'll try acupuncture."

Joni's mom was a professional acupuncturist, and Joni had recently been certified, too. It was now another alternative therapy that Heartland could offer clients, and Amy wondered if Heart's Ease might be their first success using the method. "And he's definitely had a full examination to check his temperature, urine, any swellings. . . ." She broke off at the sound of Ty chuckling. "What?"

"Listen to you! What happened to my alternative-remedies warrior?"

"Come off it, Ty. You know we always make sure the horses have been treated conventionally if there's any chance of an underlying medical problem." Amy tried to keep the edge of annoyance out of her voice.

"I was just kidding," Ty replied, his eyebrows shooting up. "You know we always call Scott to check visitors as soon as they arrive."

Amy took a deep breath. Maybe she was being a little

sensitive. "Have you asked how they keep Heart's Ease at home? If he's stabled all the time he could be totally bored with his diet. Maybe he's just longing to be let out to graze." She didn't want to say that she'd studied a similar case at college. It seemed like mentioning school created tension between them.

Ty looked thoughtful and then nodded. "It's worth a try. We've kept him in so far because his owner said he always tries to escape when he's turned out at home, so she keeps him boxed with lunging sessions or riding each day. I'll call the owner tonight and then we can turn him out in the morning."

Amy smiled up at Ty, relieved that the tension had passed. "After we do that, I'd love to put in some work with Spindle."

Ty hesitated. "I guess I forgot to mention that Joni and I decided to keep him quiet for the next few months. We're keeping him in the top paddock to rest and get a chance to build up his muscles before we start seriously working him in early summer."

"You forgot to mention it?" Amy stared at Ty until his cheeks flushed. "Well, I can see how that was easy to overlook with him being *my* horse." She couldn't keep the annoyance out of her voice. "Why didn't you check with me first? Didn't you think that I might be looking forward to working him this week?"

"I'm sorry," Ty said, "but I can't really fit Spindle's

training schedule around your college breaks." He reached out to squeeze her hand as if he was trying to stop this from becoming an argument. "You knew when you went to college that the day-to-day running of this place was being taken over by the rest of us. I know it must be hard for you coming home to find changes but there's really no way around it."

Amy knew that Ty was making sense but she was still struggling with disappointment. "I'm going to go see him now," she said. "You said he's in the top paddock? I didn't see him on the drive up to the house."

"Yeah. He was standing under the trees with Sundance the last time I saw him," Ty said helpfully. "It's really mild tonight so I decided to leave Sunny out with him for company."

As Amy left the barn, she couldn't help but notice that he hadn't offered to come with her. She sighed. She couldn't figure out why things had gotten tense between the two of them so quickly. *I'm probably just tired and blowing things out of proportion. Everything will be back to normal after I've had a good night's sleep.*

Amy leaned on the five-bar gate and shaded her eyes against the low sun. Spindleberry and Sundance were grazing side-by-side a short distance away. Amy gave a low whistle. Both horses threw up their heads and stared at her. As Spindle scented the air, Amy was suddenly worried that neither horse would want to come to her. After all, other people had taken over feeding and riding them.

Sundance dispelled her concerns with a long drawn-out whinny. He broke into a trot, easily covering the soft ground. Spindle chased after him at a rapid, gangly canter, overtaking the buckskin gelding to arrive at Amy first.

"Steady!" Amy laughed. She climbed over the gate and threw her arms around Spindle's neck. "You've grown," she said as she hugged him. When she turned to do the same to Sundance, Spindle nudged her back before lipping at her pockets. "But your manners certainly haven't improved," Amy scolded gently.

She gave them each a horse cookie, and pressed her head against theirs in turn. She'd missed them both so much. She breathed in their horsey smell and tangled her fingers in their manes. "I wish I could pack you in my suitcase and smuggle you into college. India might object to having two more roommates, though!" she told them.

Sundance's eyes were just as bright as the much younger colt's and their buckskin and dark roan coats gleamed as if they'd just been groomed.

Spindle butted Amy's hand to see if she had any more treats. "They're all gone." Amy chuckled. When Spindle grazed his tongue over Amy's palm, Sundance's ears flashed back. He swung his head at Spindle and nipped the colt's neck.

"Sunny!" Amy protested as Spindle squealed and wheeled away.

Sundance looked unrepentant as his ears came forward again and he nudged Amy's palm, looking for the treat he'd thought Spindle had been enjoying.

"You are such a bad boy," Amy scolded. Sundance had always had an unpredictable temper but he responded to Amy better than to anyone else. She thought back to the Christmas Eve years ago that she'd spent walking him around and around the yard while he was fighting off a near-fatal attack of colic. There had been several moments when she'd thought she was going to lose him. During that long, cold night an unbreakable bond had been forged between them, hammered out by fear, trust, and perseverance. Their reward had been a slip of paper in an envelope given to Amy the next day by her mother. *Sundance's bill of sale.* Amy remembered the incredible joy she'd felt as she'd raced down to the gelding's stable, knowing that he belonged to her and her alone.

"I'll take you out for a ride tomorrow," she promised him, teasing a burr out of his forelock. It would be fun to ride the familiar trails and she hoped Ty would be able to come with her. She gave Sundance a final pat and then climbed back over the gate.

As she walked back toward the main farmhouse she could see Scott's Jeep parked outside the kitchen window alongside her grandpa's car. She quickened her pace. Finally, her whole family was home!

"The wanderer returns!" Grandpa said as he put down the peeler he was using on a small mountain of potatoes and came to give Amy a hug. "It's so good to have you home, sweetheart."

"It's good to be here," she said, hugging him back.

Nancy came over to hug her, too. "We're sorry we weren't here when you arrived. We got carried away with food shopping for your welcome-home dinner."

"Lamb?" Amy inquired. But it was hardly a question. The kitchen was filled with the smell of the roast.

"With all the trimmings," Nancy declared. "I've even been persuaded to make a Baked Alaska for dessert."

Amy grinned. "They don't feed us like this at college."

"I could tell you some scary stories about my diet when I was in veterinary training." Scott appeared, smiling in the doorway between the kitchen and living room. "It's good to see you, Amy."

"You, too." She smiled, and went over to give him a hug.

"Ah, but will you still think so after a week working with me?" His eyes twinkled teasingly. "We've got normal clinic work plus an appointment to vaccinate a herd of cows over at Hollybush Farm; a cat with cardiovascular problems, a rabbit that needs neutering, a hamster that's been injured on its exercise wheel, an ex-race horse that needs physiotherapy, and Mr. Vimes's best dog, Heidi, has come down with a mysterious case of bad breath." He listed them all off on his fingers.

Amy recognized the name of the champion show dog. The black Labrador had been featured in a magazine article six months before. The dog's case brought Will suddenly to her mind, but she pushed the thought of him away and returned her focus to Scott.

"That all sounds fantastic," she said. The week was going to be busy, that was for sure!

"Great. Well, that's the plan for Monday," Scott said straight-faced, and it took Amy a few seconds to realize he was kidding.

Lou joined them from the other room and Amy noticed how quick Scott was to pull out a chair for her at the kitchen table and help her sit down.

"I don't know how you think I manage all the times you're not around," Lou told him, her smile taking the sting out of her words.

"Well, maybe Amy will be such a natural when she comes out to work with me that I can leave her to it and come back to look after you some more," Scott joked.

"Don't threaten me." Lou laughed.

Amy pulled out a chair beside her sister, glad to see that she looked a little less tired. She felt a warm glow being back with her family and with the exciting prospect of going out on Scott's rounds with him, plus getting some clinical experience. At least since they were boarding fewer horses things would be quiet in the yard and she wouldn't feel torn about leaving Ty to do all the work while she went off each morning.

"I'll go get Ty," she said as she thought of her boyfriend. She was surprised he hadn't come up to the house yet. *Maybe he thinks I need time to catch up with my family.*

She jumped to her feet and headed for the back door. When Ty joined the rest of her family, her first night back at home would be complete.

Chapter Three

Sunday was normally the only day of the week that Amy got to sleep in at school. Not remembering she'd need to get up early now that she was home, she forgot all about setting her alarm. The sun shining through her window eventually woke her up but it wasn't until she looked at her clock that she realized she should be out helping Ty with the horses. She jumped out of bed with a cry and dressed as quickly as she could, but by the time she got down to the yard, Ty was finishing up the stable chores.

"I'm so sorry!" Amy exclaimed over the noise of Ty hosing down the barn aisle. "I wanted to be here early to help out."

"It's OK." Ty nodded at the broom propped up against

one of the stall doors. "You can sweep up after me if you want."

"Sure," Amy said, picking up the broom and starting to push the water into the gutters that were on both sides of the aisle.

Ty finished hosing and went to turn off the water. "I brought Sundance in. I thought we could go for a ride on him and Harlequin."

"That sounds great." Amy still felt bad about not showing up until all of the work was done but she'd be able to help out that evening. Her work with Scott didn't start until tomorrow and, aside from some reading for school, she was free to do what she wanted for the rest of the day.

Ty got the tack while Amy finished up. When she went into Sundance's stall, the gelding nickered softly. "Yes, you know what that means, don't you?" Amy nodded at the saddle that Ty had placed on the half wall. "It means we're going out for a ride." She drew the body brush over his coat in long sweeping strokes. The dried mud came off easily, and soon Amy was tacking him up and leading him out of the barn.

Ty was already mounted on Harlequin. The chunky paint horse had come to Heartland after losing his nerve in a team jumping competition when the rider jumping in front of him had taken a fall. The horse and rider had been badly injured, and, although Harlequin had been pulled up in time to avoid a collision, the experience had left him extremely nervous whenever he was faced with a jump.

"How's his progress?" Amy asked.

"We'll be sending him home this week, I hope." Ty leaned forward to pat the gelding's neck. "He responded really well to join-up and we did a lot of flatwork with Joni riding alongside to build up his confidence of being ridden close to other horses."

Amy mounted Sundance and squeezed him forward. The gelding tossed his head and then settled into long eager strides as they headed off the yard and toward Teak's Hill. Amy leaned forward in the saddle as they made their way up the sandy trail. She could hear Ty behind them talking encouragingly to Harlequin. This was the first time the gelding had been ridden off the yard and he was doing well. The paint horse broke into a light sweat at first, but Ty kept riding gently yet firmly and before long, Harlequin unclamped his tail and pricked his ears.

"Let's see how he goes following you over some jumps," Ty called as they rode toward a turnoff from the main trail.

The previous year they had adapted a small cross-country course along the small trail. Amy knew it was an ideal place to see if Harlequin had really conquered his fears. Following Sundance closely over a course of unfamiliar fences would be a similar experience to the time he'd been on the jumping team.

She shortened her reins and turned Sundance off the main trail. His stride immediately became bouncier as he anticipated her command to canter. "Ready?" Amy called over her shoulder.

"Ready," Ty called back.

The first jump was a fallen tree that Sundance made a rather careless jump over, knocking his front legs. In response, he overjumped the next obstacle, a stream, unbalancing Amy with his exaggerated leap. *I'm out of practice,* she thought as she settled back into Sundance's rhythmic stride. She gave her full attention to the next jump — a makeshift picket fence divided into an in-and-out combination — and was rewarded with a beautiful leap from the gelding that cleared both sections easily.

Amy felt a wide grin spread across her face as Sundance put on a spurt of speed causing his mane to whip back over her hands. She slowed him reluctantly as the path dipped down into a ditch. Sundance boldly jumped onto the opposite bank before covering the uphill section in three powerful strides and heaving himself up onto the level trail.

"How did he do?" Amy asked as moments later Ty appeared on Harlequin. The paint horse was panting, and Ty gave him a long rein.

"It was a little touch-and-go at first, and he really didn't like it when you jumped the fallen tree, but I was ready for that because the accident happened at a log fence. After the first two jumps he started to relax. He's a great mover." Ty patted Harlequin's neck.

"That's fantastic." Amy was thrilled at Ty and Joni's success. At first it had been hard when she'd gone to college, knowing that horses were still coming and going from Heartland and being healed without her. *I guess everyone likes to feel irreplaceable,* Amy thought ruefully. But she knew that if Heartland had struggled without her she'd have been more devastated than anyone. The horses that were healed at Heartland were what mattered. Heartland wasn't there to feed her ego.

"I wish college were close enough for me to come home some weekends," she confessed. "I really miss riding with you."

"It's hard on us all that you're only able to come back on long vacations," Ty agreed.

What went unspoken was that it had been Amy's decision to leave and her absence affected others. Amy thought of how much more straightforward Ty's career path had been — he'd never gone to college. She often felt there was a barrier between them when she called to talk about what was going on at school. Now she tried to think of something that might interest him. "One of the guys I know at school is spending his break in Arizona. He's staying on a ranch and he's going to help out with a cattle drive at the end of the week. It sounds so cool."

"Which guy?" Ty asked as the horses began to pick their way down the track.

"Will. I told you about him before." Suddenly, Amy realized that this might not have been the best topic to bring up.

"The one who asked you to the dance?" Ty's tone was neutral.

"Yeah." Amy half-halted Sundance whose faster stride meant he was outpacing Harlequin as they rode down the path toward home. "But, like I told you at the time, I said no and told him about you."

"But you still hang out with him?" Ty leaned forward to flip a section of Harlequin's mane back on the left side of his neck.

"It's difficult not to since we're in the same program. We even got paired up to work on a project together."

"Oh." Ty sounded surprised.

"It was just some research on feline leukemia. A lot of the time we worked on it separately." She knew she sounded defensive. "He's never tried to be anything but a friend since he found out about you."

"It's fine," Ty said. "I'm not suddenly going to turn into a green-eyed monster."

"I know that." Amy smiled.

"It wouldn't be fair to the horses and I'd hate to think of how much it would set back Harlequin's progress," Ty teased, but then he grew serious again. "I don't want to stop you from having friends at college, OK?"

"OK," Amy agreed.

"Speaking of friends, I made plans for us to meet up with some people tonight," Ty continued. "I've been hanging around with some of my friends from school lately. Some of the old gang moved back into the area and we've met up a few times. Will you come meet them?"

"Sure." Amy pushed away her disappointment that Ty hadn't planned for them to be alone that night. Sundance began to jog and she half-halted him, surprised that the run hadn't taken the edge off his friskiness.

"He's not getting enough exercise," Ty commented. He dropped behind Sundance to ride single file down the narrow trail that led onto the yard. "He doesn't get ridden when you're at school. Joni and I are too big to be comfortable on him. All we're able to do is lunge him and keep him turned out as much as possible."

Amy leaned forward to pat Sundance's neck. If only she could afford to keep him in the school stables. She hated the thought of him getting bored.

"I think we should advertise for someone to ride him," Ty said, pulling out of his stirrups and jumping off

Harlequin. "Maybe someone who's still in school so they're not too heavy for him. They could come up a few times a week in the afternoon and on the weekends."

Amy felt her stomach flip over at the thought of a stranger coming to ride Sundance. What if the person riding him was heavy-handed or impatient? "I don't think a novice would work. He's too strong-willed." But she knew that Ty was right. It was only fair to Sundance for them to find someone who could ride him regularly.

"I'm sure we can find someone with some experience," Ty replied. He ran his stirrups up the back of their leathers. "We'll never get the umbilical cord cut between you and Sunny but I think we might be able to find someone he'll tolerate!"

Amy smiled. She rubbed the gelding's nose, knowing that because he was prone to colic, they had to safeguard him from anything that might trigger the condition and that meant he had to be kept in for long periods of the year when the grass was frosty. So he often had more energy than the other horses and needed to be ridden because he couldn't be turned out 24/7.

"OK, let's try to find someone," she agreed. "Maybe we could advertise before I go back." She hoped Ty wouldn't take that as a criticism that she didn't trust him to find someone on his own.

"Atta girl," Ty said. He led Harlequin into the barn.

Amy led Sundance into his stall. The palomino rubbed his head against her shoulder, itching underneath his bridle where he'd gotten sweaty.

"Do you want someone else to come ride you?" Amy murmured into his bushy ear. She sighed. Ty only had Heartland's best interests in mind and she appreciated his concern about Sundance. But it made her wonder if she'd ever get used to decisions being made without her. Not for the first time she wished she could split herself into two. *But since that's never going to happen I need to get used to the fact that someone else needs to be making judgment calls. And I can't think of anyone better than Ty to do that.*

❧

After lunch, Amy decided to give Soraya a call. She was excited that they would actually have a chance to talk. Within minutes, the conversation turned to Soraya's new boyfriend, Anthony. "He's the most amazing musician," Soraya enthused. "I never liked jazz before but I'm really getting into it now."

"I can't wait to meet him. Have you still been staying in touch with Matt?" Amy knew Soraya wouldn't mind being asked about her ex. Amy and Matt had been best friends before they dated for a while. She was glad that their breakup had been amicable. In fact, Soraya was often the first to bring up his name.

"I e-mailed him last week to see if he wanted to get together but he's not coming home," Soraya replied. "He's doing some research project for extra credit and hasn't got the time to leave campus."

Amy wasn't surprised; whenever Scott talked about his younger brother, he said how totally wrapped up in his pre-med studies Matt was.

"So do you want to come over tonight?" Soraya asked. "We could do the whole girls'-night-in thing and rent a DVD, eat mountains of popcorn . . ."

"I'm really sorry, but I've already got plans," Amy apologized. "Ty and I are going to meet up with a bunch of his old school-friends."

"So he wants to show off his hotshot veterinarian girl-friend?" Soraya teased. "You'll probably end up doing a question-and-answer session on their pets' ailments."

"Great! That's just how I want to spend my night out," Amy said with a laugh.

"Maybe not, but you sound like you've come a long way at school. I'm so proud of you," Soraya told her.

"Straight back at you, Beatrice," Amy told her friend, referencing Soraya's leading role in her college's pro-duction of *Much Ado About Nothing*. She was planning on going to watch her in the opening night performance next month. "I've still got a lot to learn, but I'm loving every minute of the program, even though it's intense with a capital *I*."

"It feels weird coming home right in the middle of everything, huh?" Soraya asked.

"It does take some adjusting to," Amy admitted. She looked out of the kitchen window across the empty yard. "I guess it's just hard coming home and not finding things the way I remember them. I mean, the stable is only half full, Spindle's being rested so I can't work him, Joni's on vacation, Lou's about to have the baby, and Ty . . ." She paused. Ty was exactly the same, wasn't he?

"How *is* Lou?" Soraya asked, ignoring Amy's hesitation over her boyfriend. "She's only got a couple of months left to go now, right? I wish someone in my family would have a baby, it would be so cool to be an aunt." She hesitated. "Although I guess I couldn't be too involved while I'm away at college. And my mom treats *me* like a kid when I'm home on vacation. She told me to go to bed at ten last night! I had to tell her that's usually what time my evening gets started!"

Amy smiled. "Soraya, I've got to run. Maybe we can get together later on this week?"

"Sure, have fun tonight," Soraya told her before hanging up.

Amy headed up to her room. Suddenly, she knew exactly what she was going to do. She was going to put an amazing outfit together to show Ty there were definite benefits to having a college girlfriend!

❧

Amy carefully darkened her upper eyelid with a deep shade of blue that emphasized the grayness of her eyes. "Oh, what the heck," she murmured, picking up her mascara. She might as well go for the total wow factor.

She stood back from her mirror to check out the effect of her thin-strapped glittery top and denim skirt. She'd decided to put her hair up and, with the boots she was wearing, she figured she'd look almost as tall as Ty. She picked up her purse and switched off the light. Grandpa and Nancy had gone to the movies but Ty had shouted up a few minutes ago to say he was waiting for her in the kitchen.

"Hey, you look" — Ty paused for a moment when Amy appeared in the doorway — "really good."

"Thanks. You look nice, too." Amy felt a little disappointed by Ty's muted reaction after she'd made such an effort. She also felt a little overdressed beside him because he was wearing a plaid shirt and jeans.

"Where are we meeting your friends?" she asked as they walked out to Ty's car.

"Jefferson's, on the other side of town," Ty told her. "It's where we usually hang out to shoot some pool and listen to live music. They get some really cool bands playing there."

"That sounds great," Amy said. It wasn't her usual

scene, but she guessed it could be fun, especially since she'd be with Ty.

Jefferson's was a new restaurant on the outskirts of town just a ten-minute drive away. They pulled up to the sound of music blaring through the open doors where there were groups of people hanging around to listen. It was quite warm for late March and everyone was making the most of the weather.

When Amy walked with Ty into the dark building, her heart sank. Everyone was dressed casually, with most of the girls wearing T-shirts and jeans. *How out of place am I?*

In the back was a smaller room where she caught a glimpse of pool tables. Ty began to negotiate his way toward it, skirting the small square dance floor that was already crowded. One of the boys enthusiastically bouncing to the live performance stumbled back and bumped into Amy who wasn't quick enough to avoid him.

"Sorry," he apologized.

Ty turned to take her hand. "It's hard to believe there's a single guy in here that didn't notice you walk in wearing that outfit," he teased. "Are you OK?"

Amy nodded. Didn't Ty know that she already felt awkward enough without him drawing attention to the fact that she was overdressed? He should have said something earlier so she could have changed.

Her cheeks were still burning when Ty began to

introduce the crowd of people at one of the pool tables. "This is JJ, Miranda, Andy, Jono, Ali, and Ella. Guys, this is Amy."

Amy smiled, knowing that she didn't have a prayer of remembering all their names. "I should have brought my sticky labels to make some name tags!" she joked.

"Hey, Amy, can I get you a soda?" asked a boy with black curly hair. Amy thought he was Jono.

"It's okay, I'll go get a pitcher of Coke," Ty offered. "I'll be right back."

"So, Amy, you're home for spring break, huh?" Miranda asked after Ty had gone. She had the most piercing blue eyes Amy had ever seen. The girl began chalking her cue while she waited for Amy to reply.

"Right," Amy nodded. "I guess Ty's told you a little about me?"

"You mean, what *hasn't* Ty told us about his college girl-friend?" drawled the blond girl standing alongside Jono.

"That sounds ominous." She laughed. "I just hope you got the edited highlights!"

A slightly awkward silence followed, interrupted by Ty returning with a large pitcher of soda and eight glasses. "Hey guys, rack up the balls!"

"I want to dance before we play. Come on, Ty, the others can set up," the blond girl declared.

Ty shot Amy a glance as the girl grabbed his hand and tried to tug him toward the dance floor. "No thanks,

Ella," Ty said quietly. Ella looked at him a moment longer before shrugging and heading out to the front room.

"Don't worry about Ella," said Miranda, who had obviously noticed Amy's surprised reaction. "She's got a major crush on Ty but everyone knows he hasn't got eyes for anyone except you. He's so proud of how well you're doing in college."

Amy felt herself go red with pleasure. "Oh, yeah?" she said, giving Ty a playful look. He just rolled his eyes and smiled back.

"Totally," the brunette called Ali joined in. Amy knew the girls were trying to be friendly but she still felt uncomfortable.

She was saved from replying by the ring of her cell phone. She looked down at the screen and saw Will's name.

"I'm going to take this outside," she excused herself before hurrying out of the restaurant. She knew Ty was watching her leave but she made a point of avoiding his gaze. Once she made it to the relative quiet of the parking lot, she flipped open her phone.

"Hey, Amy," Will said as soon as she answered. "I was starting to think you were screening your calls!"

"Are you kidding? It's really good to hear from you." Amy was surprised to realize how much she meant it. "How's Arizona?"

"I'm thinking of quitting college and becoming a cowboy," Will joked. "I've just about mastered the bowlegged walk and I'm now perfecting the art of consuming inhuman quantities of food."

Amy laughed. "Now I know why I came home for spring break. It was to recover from your awful sense of humor!"

"Ouch," Will said with a chuckle. "So, I bet you're having a great time back at home with your family, not to mention all those horses to cure?"

Amy hesitated. She was, of course she was. *It will be better when I start working with Scott.*

"Amy?"

Amy realized she hadn't answered Will. She was about to tell him that everything was great, but instead the truth came out. "It's kind of weird right now," she admitted. "I guess I expected things to be exactly how I left them. I should have known that wouldn't happen."

Will paused. "I'm sorry to hear that. I don't know if it will help or not if I confess things aren't exactly what I expected here, either. I wasn't prepared to be the proverbial stranger in a strange land. All the ranch hands have this sort of club going on that doesn't give out temporary membership. And other people who have come to help out with the drive have come as part of a group." He gave a quick laugh.

"It's not exactly fun when reality turns out to be different from your expectations, huh?" Amy said softly.

She was about to go on when she saw Ty walk out of the restaurant and scan the parking lot for her. "Will, I've got to go, sorry."

"Oh, OK." Will sounded disappointed.

"I'll talk to you soon," Amy said before hanging up.

"Who was that on the phone?" Ty asked.

Amy wondered if he would suspect there was something going on if she told him Will had called her. Before she even realized what she was doing, she replied, "Grandpa was wondering if I needed a ride home." She avoided looking Ty in the eye by concentrating on putting her phone back into her purse. Grandpa *had* asked earlier on if she needed a ride, but she immediately wished she'd just told Ty it was Will who had called. There was nothing to hide.

Ty raised his eyebrows. "You didn't tell Jack you're with me? Is this your way of hinting that you want to go home?"

"No!" Amy said quickly, noting the look of relief flash across Ty's face. It was clear he wasn't ready to leave.

She deliberately put her arms around Ty's neck. "Let's go back in and play pool."

Ty grinned. "Now you're talking."

As they headed back inside Amy tried to ignore the feeling that she wasn't being honest with Ty like he deserved. It shouldn't be Will she was unburdening herself to, it should be her boyfriend. She slipped her hand into his. From now on, she was going to be one hundred percent open with Ty. This week was going to be over too quickly and she didn't want to waste time playing games.

Chapter Four

Amy's stomach rumbled as she walked into the kitchen and smelled fresh blueberry muffins. "Someone's been busy," she said, smiling at her grandpa.

Jack looked up from where he was reading the morning newspapers in his favorite chair. "How did it go this morning? I bet you didn't have any breakfast before you left with Scott."

"It went really well, thanks," Amy said, pulling back a crisp white napkin covering two muffins. She wasn't being totally honest. Although she'd enjoyed following Scott on his rounds and helping him with his work, none of it had been quite demanding enough to take her mind off wishing she was back at Heartland helping in the yard. They had treated a dog for ticks, vaccinated a small herd of cows, examined a cat that had breathing problems, and clipped a rabbit's nails. It had been interesting meeting Scott's clients but she hadn't been able to stop thinking about what they could do to tempt Heart's Ease to eat, and how they could boost Harlequin's confidence when he was on a trail.

She had promised to spend the afternoon shopping with Lou but she hoped there'd be enough time when she got back to help with the evening yard routine. Still, Amy was looking forward to helping pick out baby clothes and bedlinens to match the beautiful yellow-painted nursery at Lou's house.

"Lou called just before you walked in to say she'd be over in twenty minutes," Jack told her.

"Is it twelve already?" Amy exclaimed, looking at the clock. She grabbed the second muffin and headed for the door. "I'd better hurry up and get changed."

She quickly washed and then tugged on a fresh pair of jeans and a clean T-shirt. She brushed her long brown hair and was pulling it into a ponytail when she heard Lou's car pull up and honk. Amy rushed to put on some lip gloss and grabbed her purse off the back of her chair.

"Hi, how are you doing today?" Amy called as she ran out to Lou's car. "Whoa! If your bump gets any bigger you're not going to be able to turn the steering wheel!"

"Thanks for pointing that out, Amy. I was feeling totally svelte until just now," Lou said with a smirk.

"I bet you can't wait for the baby to come," Amy said sympathetically as she reached for her seat belt.

"Counting the days," Lou agreed.

When they got into town, Lou parked near the boutique where she'd bought her wedding dress.

I can't believe how quickly things happen. It feels like only a couple of weeks ago we were here, trying on our dresses, Amy thought as she got out of the car.

There was a baby store a few doors down from the wedding dress shop and it was having a half-price sale. Lou and Amy went in to buy a few onesies and bibs, but somehow managed to fill an entire basket with beautiful satin dresses, adorable teddy-bear-print pj's, and the most gorgeous crib that Lou said would break her entire baby budget but was totally worth it.

When they stopped for a snack, Amy couldn't resist stroking the soft faux-fur lining of the crib, imagining her new niece snuggled inside.

"Scott and I have finally settled on a name," Lou said, picking carefully at the brownie she'd gotten.

"Really?" Amy knew they had been making a list of favorites for their daughter. "What have you decided?"

"Holly Marion," Lou said softly.

"That's beautiful." As Amy replied, she felt her throat tighten. Their mom's memory was kept alive in so many ways at Heartland but this had to be the most special of all. Her mom would have been so thrilled to have had a granddaughter, and now baby Holly Marion would carry her name as well. "Mom would already be planning to get Holly in the saddle." Amy smiled, blinking back tears.

"Well, we each have photos of us being held on ponies at a few months old, so maybe when you're home on your summer vacation you can do the honors." Lou reached out to squeeze Amy's hand. "It's becoming a tradition."

"A Fleming tradition," Amy murmured and then corrected herself. "Trewin. I keep forgetting you're not a Fleming now that you're married to Scott."

Lou smiled at the mention of her husband's name. "He's going to make a wonderful father, I just know it. He's been so great throughout the pregnancy. He's been to all of my doctor's appointments, he's always calling to check up on me, and he won't let me do anything around the house. Although I'm not sure how many times I can face eating either pizza or chicken stir-fry for dinner. He thinks I haven't noticed that that's all he can cook!" She laughed and then spoke more seriously. "He knows what I want even before I do some of the time. He's amazing."

Amy flicked a few grains of sugar off the table. "It must be great to be with someone who knows you so well."

Lou looked at Amy and frowned. "I kind of thought you *are* with someone like that. Is everything OK with you and Ty?"

"Would you believe me if I said everything's fine?" Amy made an attempt to smile but couldn't manage it.

"I hadn't really given it any thought until now. I mean, you and Ty have been together for so long," Lou replied. She leaned in and made a point of meeting Amy's eyes. "What's going on?"

"That's the thing. I don't know," Amy admitted. "I just know that things aren't the way they were; the way I think they *should* be. It feels like I have to think before I do or say anything and it never used to be that way. And the stupid thing is that I was really looking forward to coming home for spring break and spending time with Ty."

Lou sighed. "You didn't think this might happen when you went away?"

Amy felt alarm shoot through her. "What do you mean? Nothing has happened! I just need some time to readjust after being away at college."

Lou looked down at her fingernails. "Maybe." She didn't sound convinced. "Don't hate me for what I'm about to say, but have you thought about taking a break from each other?"

Amy felt sick. "All I said was that things weren't quite right and you're jumping straight to us splitting up?" She couldn't accept the idea of breaking up with Ty. He was a part of everything that was important in her life.

"Amy, if I'd met Scott in high school do you think I'd

have ended up marrying him? I was such a different person back then. I'm not saying that Ty isn't right for you. I'm saying that maybe you're not right together at this time in your lives. All you've known so far is Heartland, but there's a far bigger world out there."

"I don't think I want to talk about this anymore." Amy pushed away her plate and looked down at the Claddagh ring Ty had given her. It was an ancient Irish symbol of love and friendship. When the tiny pair of hands holding a silver heart faced outward it meant your heart was free, but if it was facing in it meant your heart belonged to someone. When he had given it to her, Amy had told Ty that her heart would always belong to him. Going away to college wouldn't change what they had. Lou was right about there being a far bigger world than Heartland to experience, but she was wrong if she thought Amy would ever want anything else.

When Amy got out of the car she decided to go straight down to the barn to find Ty. She needed to be with him. A note in Ty's handwriting was pinned to the main doors. *Ran out of cod liver oil, went to get some more.*

Disappointed, she decided to do some of Ty's work so he'd be free when he got back. She went to the desk in the feed room and opened the file to check the week's schedule. This afternoon, Bunny, a white-and-gray mare, was due to be exercised. Amy didn't read up on her admission notes because Ty had already mentioned that Bunny would be ready to go home at the end of the week. Amy figured she'd school the mare in one of the arenas and then take her over a small course of jumps.

She collected Bunny's tack and left it in her stall while she went to the turnout paddocks to catch her. "Not you!" She laughed as Spindle cantered up, as if he hoped she was coming to work him. "Enjoy your time off, it won't last long."

Bunny was easy to catch and stood patiently while Amy groomed and tacked her up. When Amy went to pull out her front legs to make her comfortable under the girth the mare actually held out each foreleg. "Where did you come from, the circus?" Amy teased.

Down in the arena she rode Bunny through all of the basic school movements. The mare had nice easy paces as she went from walk to trot to canter. Amy did some gentle leg-yielding across the school and again, Bunny obeyed without hesitation. Amy felt she was something of a push-button horse but without any pizzazz. "Let's see if some jumps light your fire," she said, clicking with her tongue as they rode into the jumping arena.

There was already a course of six low jumps set out, and Bunny pricked her ears as Amy encouraged her into a canter. She gave a small buck when Amy set her at the first fence, a cross pole. *This is more like it,* Amy thought as they landed and she had to slow Bunny. The mare swished her tail as she cantered toward the next jump. The upright was a lot higher and narrower than the first fence and Amy had to half-halt Bunny to get her to listen. The mare took off too soon and hit the top pole hard.

"Amy! Stop!"

Amy pulled on Bunny's reins and looked over to the gate where Ty was waving his arms.

"Get off!" He sounded unnecessarily upset.

Has he totally lost it? We just hit a rail, that's all. Amy stared at Ty as he ran across and grabbed Bunny's bridle.

Ty's eyes were dark with anger. "Why were you jumping her? She's not ready."

"What do you mean, she's not ready? You told me she's going home this week," Amy retorted.

"Didn't you read her notes? Bunny hasn't come to us for reschooling, she's here to recover from an injury!" Ty glared up at Amy. "You've probably set her back a week!"

Amy took off her stirrups and slid off Bunny. She felt awful. Why hadn't she taken the time to read Bunny's history? "What's wrong with her?"

"She sprained her shoulder when she rolled in her field at home. Her owners were in the middle of moving so they left her with us to recover in the meantime. She was supposed to be going home this week ready to be worked gently, which doesn't involve being ridden over a course of fences!"

Amy felt her stomach churn as she watched Ty run his hand over Bunny's shoulder and down her leg. "Walk her forward," he told Amy quietly.

The moment Bunny began to move Amy could tell she was unhappy about putting weight on her leg.

"Lame. Great. Thanks." Ty walked across to take Bunny's reins out of Amy's hands.

He doesn't even trust me to hold her, Amy thought miserably.

She followed them back up to the yard. "I'll go and get the hose," she told Ty when he led the gray-and-white mare into her stall.

Ty nodded but didn't look at her as he started to untack Bunny.

Amy returned with the hose and began to spray water over Bunny's shoulder, watching the mare quietly accept the cold jet with only a flick of her ears. Amy bit her lip. Bunny had such a lovely trusting nature. She didn't deserve to have this setback. *And it's all my fault.* Feeling close to tears, she didn't notice Ty was watching her until he came to stand close beside her.

"I'm sorry I lost my temper with you," he said. "I shouldn't have snapped at you like that."

"Yes, you should have," Amy replied, not taking her

eyes off Bunny's leg. "It was stupid of me not to read her case notes. Some vet I'm going to be."

Ty slipped his arms around her waist. "You're going to be an amazing vet," he reassured her. "Everyone's allowed to make mistakes."

"Not when it's animals who have to pay the price." Amy wouldn't go as easy on herself as Ty.

"I'm going to have to go call Bunny's owners and postpone her homecoming." Ty changed the subject. "I might as well admit we pushed her a little too far."

Amy winced at the thought of Heartland's reputation being damaged by her stupid oversight. "Do you think it's a good idea to tell them everything? Why don't you just say that she did it when she was cantering in the paddock?"

Ty dropped his arms and stepped away from her. "I'm not going to lie, Amy."

Amy felt her cheeks begin to burn. What was going on with her? She'd always been open and honest and yet yesterday she'd told Ty Grandpa was on the phone and not Will, and here she was again, wanting to bend the truth to protect Heartland's reputation.

"That might be the way you're taught to handle clients in college, but it's not something I'll ever do." Ty's tone was edged like a knife.

Amy turned the nozzle on the hose to stop the spray

and spun around to face him. "It was a crazy suggestion. Just forget about it, OK? Pretend I never said it."

She knew Ty well enough to sense that he was struggling to let it go, but he nodded and made a visible effort to change the subject. "So, did you have fun last night?"

Not really, were the words that rushed into Amy's head but she held them back. She stepped over to Bunny and ran her hand over her shoulder and down her leg, noting that despite the hosing the muscle felt tight. *I'll have to bandage her to give her extra support and help with the discomfort.*

"Amy?" Ty prompted.

She straightened up. "Your friends are great. I can see why you like hanging out with them." *I'm not lying, I'm being diplomatic.* The truth was, Ty fit in with them really well and they had made a real effort to include Amy. *But his friends are so different from me; I just didn't click with them.* At least Ty didn't seem to notice how uncomfortable she had felt.

"I'm really glad you liked them. I guess it meant more to me than I thought," Ty admitted. He pushed his hair off his forehead. "While we're on the subject, Ella's asked a favor."

Amy stiffened. "What?"

"She asked if there's any part-time work for her to do

here. She'd fit it in around the shifts she works at Scott's clinic."

Amy felt an icy coldness in the pit of her stomach. *She's totally trying to move in on Ty and he can't even see it.* Then a worse thought occurred. *What if Ty can see it and he doesn't mind? Maybe he even likes it.*

The ice in her stomach turned to cramping pains. "What did you have in mind?" She was amazed at how even her tone was.

"She could take over the office work until Lou's ready to come back, and I thought she could exercise Sundance when you're away. She's light enough and I know that she's got riding experience."

So basically, she can come take over my horse, my home, and my boyfriend. Over my dead body! Amy took a deep breath. "Let me think about it. I'm going to go get some support bandages for Bunny."

"I don't see what there is to think about. Why can't I just tell her yes?" Ty sounded exasperated as Amy headed for the door.

"What part of 'I'll think about it' don't you understand?" Amy snapped as she fought the temptation to slam the stall door shut.

Marching down to the tack room, she found it hard to breathe with all the emotions battling inside her. Spring break was just not turning out the way she had planned!

Chapter Five

As soon as Amy had made Bunny comfortable she went to call her best friend.

"Hey, Soraya. Do you want to get together tonight?" she asked when her friend picked up.

"That would be great, but aren't you doing something with Ty?" Soraya replied.

Amy gave a short sarcastic laugh.

"I see. How soon do you want to come over?" Soraya's voice was full of concern.

"I'll get Grandpa to drop me off after I get changed." As far as Amy was concerned, she couldn't get to her friend soon enough. She still couldn't believe Ty's suggestion about Ella working at Heartland.

"I'll get the popcorn started," Soraya told her. "See you soon."

Amy pulled on a pair of jeans and went to find her grandfather, who was mowing the side lawn.

"Give me five minutes to finish up and then we can go," he agreed. "Is everything OK? You look a little flustered."

"It's probably all the work I'm doing instead of sitting in lecture halls. I must be out of shape," Amy teased. She'd calmed down since her phone call to Soraya and started to wonder if she might be overreacting. Ty would never cheat on her, and OK, so what if Ella found him attractive? She should just take that as a compliment. *But I'm still not sure I can say yes to Ella working at Heartland.*

She put the mower away for her grandpa while he swapped his overalls for a shirt and khakis. Amy whistled when he came back outside. "Nancy's a lucky lady."

"That's good because I often think the luck's all mine," Jack admitted.

"She's a lovely person," Amy agreed, climbing into her grandpa's pickup. "But then again, so are you!"

"You're biased," her grandpa told her as he started the engine. But Amy could tell he was flattered by the way the tips of his ears had turned red.

"So, Grandpa, isn't it about time you and Nancy tied the knot? She did such a great job helping to arrange Lou's wedding, just think of what she could organize for the two of you!" Amy was amused to see her grandpa's blush deepen and spread.

"Since when did you get interested in weddings? Wasn't Lou's enough for a few years?" Jack protested.

"Are you kidding? How could we possibly have too many weddings?"

They rode in comfortable silence after that. When they pulled up outside Soraya's house, Amy leaned over to kiss her grandpa on the cheek. "In all seriousness, I think it would be great to make Nancy an official part of our Heartland family. Think about it."

"I'll make you a deal," Jack said, his eyes twinkling. "You get out of my pickup and stop badgering me about wedding plans, and I'll give some serious thought to what you said. How's that?"

Amy pretended to consider it for a moment. "Deal," she agreed, holding out her hand to shake before scrambling out of the truck.

"I'll pick you up on my way back from Nancy's. Have fun tonight," he called through his window.

"You, too!" Amy waved and then hurried up to Soraya's front door.

Her friend was already waiting. "It feels like I haven't seen you in years! I missed you sooo much. Do you know how much catching up we have to do? I ordered a pizza and got a DVD, but it doesn't matter if we don't have time to watch it. . . ."

"Woah! Easy, girl," Amy laughed, hugging Soraya.

"Sorry." Soraya grinned. "It's just so great to see you.

Christmas break feels like it was years ago, not months." She led the way into the den where she had put out bowls of chips and popcorn.

They sat down on the comfy terracotta-colored sofa. Amy tucked up her legs and took a handful of chips from the bowl Soraya offered. "Mmm. My roommate and I must have eaten our way through a truckload of chips this last semester. Late-night snacking is way too easy when you live with another girl."

"Your roommate's India, right?" Soraya threw a chip up into the air and caught it in her mouth. "The ditzy one."

"She's OK once you get past her fashion fixation," Amy defended her roommate. "In fact, she's even persuaded me that sometimes there's more to dressing than just a T-shirt and jeans."

"Amy Fleming dressing up? I don't believe it!" Soraya pretended to gasp. "Although you *did* clean up nicely for your sister's wedding. Ty couldn't take his eyes off you." She hesitated. "Do you want to tell me what the deal is with the two of you? Your phone call kinda freaked me out."

"I think I might have overreacted," Amy confessed. "I'll tell you about it once you give me the lowdown on the new love of your life."

"Anthony." Soraya looked upward and smiled. "Oh, my gosh, Amy, he is so totally amazing. He's got the greatest sense of humor. When we're together, all we do is laugh. And he's so romantic. I didn't tell you, but last week he sent me this helium balloon with the words 'Missing you already' on it."

"He does sound pretty amazing," Amy admitted. "And he's cute, too." Soraya had e-mailed her pictures of Anthony and with his thick black hair and large dark eyes, Amy could see why her friend was smitten with her new boyfriend. "Sounds like he could be The One," she teased, smiling at the way Soraya's face quickly looked like it was on fire.

"Did I say I'd missed you? I'm starting to change my mind." Soraya threw a cushion at her. "Anyway, tell me about Ty. What's going on with you two?"

"I'm not sure." Amy hugged her knees to her chest. "We've had a couple of little arguments since I've been back, but apart from that, nothing's officially changed between us. I really thought we'd pick up where we left off — it's not like we haven't been in touch practically every day, and he knows I'm only studying so we can offer an even broader range of treatments at Heartland. And yet, at the same time, *something* is different. I just don't know what it is." She hesitated. "I guess it doesn't help that he's been hanging out with a girl who has a major crush on him. I feel like Ty was bothered by Will asking me out and yet it's totally fine that a girl is clearly hitting on him."

Amy waited for her friend to tell her that there was

nothing to worry about, but Soraya didn't say anything nearly that comforting.

"Tell me you and Ty aren't breaking up!" Soraya's eyes widened.

"You and Matt didn't make it," Amy pointed out, feeling stung.

"Oh, come on, Amy. You can't begin to compare my relationship with Matt to you and Ty. You guys are soulmates!" Soraya looked totally serious as she ditched her bowl of chips and leaned forward to grab Amy's hand. "You two go together like peanut butter and jelly!"

Amy rolled her eyes. "Can't you come up with a more romantic comparison?"

"I was going to say Romeo and Juliet but I didn't want to associate you with a couple doomed to be tragic," Soraya confessed. "You two really are made for each other. Where else are you going to find someone who understands horses the way you do?"

A picture of Will appeared in Amy's mind, talking softly to Ashia before helping to bandage her leg. She shook herself. This wasn't the time to be thinking about her college friend. "The way you're putting it makes it sound a little too intense," she replied evasively. Soraya seemed to be suggesting that no matter what Amy's opinion or feelings were, she had to remain with Ty. *What is wrong with me? Lou suggests we take a break and I go*

*ballistic, but now I'm feeling the same way about Soraya saying
we have to stay together. What do I really want?*

Amy noticed that the lines in Soraya's forehead were
deepening. "Hey, we'll be fine, I'm sure," she said lightly.
"Besides, you should be concentrating on the love of
your life."

As she'd hoped, the reference to Anthony distracted
Soraya. "Ah, *l'amour,*" she said, dramatically clasping her
hands over her heart. "Hopefully, by the end of the spring
break you'll be back to feeling Cupid's arrow, too."

Amy tried not to laugh but gave up. "Who are you and
what have you done with my best friend?" She collapsed
into giggles. "Do they teach you to talk this way in your
drama classes?"

"What way?" Soraya pretended to look wounded but
quickly joined in with Amy's laughter. "And this is before
I even get to the end of my first year. Just think how
wonderfully dramatic I'll be by the time I graduate, *dah-
ling.* I'll be ready to take my place effortlessly among
Hollywood's A-listers."

"Beverly Hills, watch out." Amy grinned. "Speaking
of which, are we really going to watch a movie?"

Soraya shook her head. "Personally, I don't think any
blockbuster will be more interesting than what we've
got to talk about."

Amy agreed, but if she had to choose between watching drama and living it, she knew which one she'd go for.

❧

Amy didn't sleep very well that night and was relieved when the sun finally peeked through her curtains. Throwing off her covers, she tugged on her work clothes and crept out of the house. It was a couple of hours before she was due to start her work with Scott, and she figured she could get to most of the chores before Ty arrived.

The first thing Amy did was check on Bunny. "I know I'm early," she whispered, kneeling down beside the mare on her deep bed of straw. "I'll go get your breakfast soon to make up for it." As she was talking, she ran her hand over the injured shoulder and skimmed her leg. To her relief the heat was already diminishing and Bunny's skin only felt warm, not hot, to the touch. "This time next week you'll be home I bet," Amy murmured, rubbing Bunny's nose. The mare sighed and rested her head on Amy's knees. "Let me up, sleepyhead." She chuckled. "I've got chores to do."

As much as she wanted to say hello to each and every horse, Amy made herself go straight to the feed room. It was more important to her to finish the stable work before Ty arrived. *I haven't exactly been the greatest help around here since getting back.*

She carefully measured out each horse's feed. "Hey, Sunny, breakfast time," she called, taking the pony his bucket. Sundance scrambled to his feet and nickered to her. Amy stood for a while just watching Sundance eat. When she ran her hand down his neck, his skin quivered like a fly had landed on him. "OK, I get the message. You want to be left to eat in peace."

She went back to giving out the rest of the feed and then began the mucking out. By the time Ty arrived, she was in the middle of stacking the rinsed-out feed buckets.

"Wow, so much for sleeping in, huh?" he said appreciatively. "Thanks, Amy."

"You bet." She smiled up at him, glad that he didn't seem to be holding a grudge for the way she'd snapped at him the day before.

"Do you want to ride Harlequin when you get back from your rounds with Scott? He's going home tomorrow, and I'd like to see how he does with a lighter rider on him."

Amy nodded. "I'd love to."

Ty picked up two halters. "And, at the risk of working you to death, can you help bring Heart's Ease and Spindle up for their morning feed? You were right on with your diagnosis with Heart's Ease, by the way. He's doing much better since being turned out. When I called his owner about it she told me that their turn-out area for Heart's Ease is a training ring, not a paddock, which would explain why he always tries to jump out."

"He was trying to get to the nearest grazing area."

Amy knew that some horses were fine being fed just hay and hard feed, but Heart's Ease was obviously bored with the diet. "Did his owner say she could get access to grazing for him?"

Ty nodded. "She's arranging to lease a nearby field from a local farmer."

"Perfect." Amy was pleased for the gelding. "If only all of our horses' problems were solved so easily!"

Ty reached out and squeezed her hand. "It was only easy because you knew the right solution."

Amy felt happiness flood over her. She didn't know why she'd thought things weren't right between the two of them. *I wish I hadn't said anything to Soraya last night. Everything's going to be fine.*

"I'm sorry I pushed you yesterday about Ella. I should have respected that you needed to think it through," Ty said as they walked out of the barn.

Amy felt herself tense at the mention of Ella's name. "I just don't think that we should give the job to the first person who comes along," she said carefully.

"It's not the first person." Ty paused before continuing. "We advertised for Lou's job and no one was right."

Amy stopped walking. "What? When did you do that? Why didn't anyone tell me?"

Ty turned to face her. He placed his hands on her waist and spoke gently. "We didn't want to worry you. But Lou's getting to the point where she really needs someone to take over. She'll have to train her replacement before she leaves, and she must be starting to feel the pressure now that there's not long before the baby arrives."

Amy instantly felt completely selfish. Why hadn't she thought about it from Lou's point of view? She took a deep breath. "Tell Ella we'll give her a trial run. If Sundance likes her, and she manages to fit Lou's work in around her shifts at Scott's clinic, then I guess she can have the job."

"I'll call her now," Ty said. "She'll be psyched."

Amy pushed away her discomfort at the prospect of having Ella at Heartland. Other people's needs, especially Lou's, had to be considered.

As they began to walk across the yard again, the kitchen door opened and Lou came out. "Your phone's ringing," she called, waving Amy's cell.

"I'll catch up with you," Amy told Ty, handing him her halter.

"It's OK, I'll wait. I've somehow ended up with a fair amount of free time this morning." He smiled and twirled the halters in each hand.

Amy took the phone from her sister. "Hello?"

"Hey, Amy, it's me. Sorry to bother you again." It was Will sounding surprisingly serious.

Amy shot a wary glance at Ty who was still clowning around with the halters. "Is everything OK?"

"Not really. I could use some advice," he admitted.

"I'm listening," Amy told him.

"It's about one of the ranch quarterhorses here. He's a great horse — you know the type, always looking out to say hello to you when you walk by?"

Amy thought of Spindle and the way he followed her every move with his dark brown eyes. "I know the type," she agreed.

"Well, Loup, that's the horse, was attacked a while back by a mountain lion when he was out on a trail ride. He got pretty torn up. His rider jumped off and climbed a tree and left Loup to make a run for it. The really bad thing, though, is that Loup galloped into a closed canyon and got mauled. The guys here think it was a female lion protecting her cubs. By the time Loup's rider got down from his tree, followed them into the canyon, and fired his gun to frighten away the lion, Loup's quarters and side had been pretty much ripped apart."

"Poor Loup," Amy whispered. What a terrible trauma for the horse to be both abandoned by his rider and then ferociously attacked.

"Tell me about it," Will agreed. "The thing is, his rider tried to get on him for the first time again last night and Loup went crazy. There's nothing physically wrong with him anymore apart from his scars, but he went bonkers when the rider tried to mount him."

"How bonkers?"

Will was silent for a moment before replying. "The guy got thrown so badly we were all afraid he broke his back."

Amy gasped. "Is he going to be all right?"

"We haven't heard too much yet about how serious it is, but his brother works here, too, and has filled us in a little. I guess he'll be in the hospital for a couple of days, and he should be all right eventually. But he's not why I'm calling." He took a deep breath. "They're talking about putting Loup down. I think it's the wrong thing to do. I've got this gut feeling that he doesn't want to hurt anyone, he's just scared. Does that make sense?"

"Totally," Amy said softly, her heart going out to the unknown quarterhorse.

Will spoke again. "Actually, Amy, I wasn't totally honest with you at the start of the call. I'm not really phoning for advice. I'm calling to see if you could come out here and save Loup before he's put down." His voice was husky with emotion. "Will you help?"

Chapter Six

"Of course I'll help." Amy's response was automatic. *Poor Loup!* Amy thought. *And the poor guy who tried to ride him.* She could understand why the quarterhorse was under threat of being put down but if that happened, it would be a double tragedy.

She noticed Ty looking questioningly at her and realized that she had some people to talk to before agreeing to help. "Will, can I call you back in a while? I'm going to need to talk this through with Ty and my family."

"Sure. I hope I haven't backed you into a corner with this," Will said apologetically.

"No, it's fine. I'm glad you thought of me," Amy reassured him. "I'll call back as soon as I've talked things through with everyone here."

"Is there anything I can do for Loup?" Will asked.

"Stay with him as much as you can without crowding him. It sounds as if he's got some real issues with trust, so he's going to be torn between wanting to have company, which is a natural instinct, and not wanting people around because he associates them with fear and pain," Amy explained. Although it sounded as if Loup didn't have a problem with people so much as with being ridden. The horse needed Bach Flower Remedies to help him with the trauma from which he clearly hadn't recovered. *And he needs to join up in order to regain his trust. The poor boy was abandoned by his rider, then attacked by a mountain lion and finally, when his rider returns, it's to fire a gun at him! No wonder he can't deal with the idea of anybody getting on his back!*

She switched off her phone and met Ty's quizzical gaze. "Can we take a break from the horses for now? I've got something I need to talk to you about."

"Don't tell me. It's an urgent case and one that you really feel can't possibly be turned down," Ty said as they walked into the farmhouse. He gave a pretend sigh. "Go ahead. Give me the details. I'm sure we can find some way of taking in another horse!"

Amy appreciated that Ty would take on an emergency case even though they were short-staffed and she struggled to find the right words to straighten out the picture for him. Loup wasn't going to be shipped all the way to

Heartland — Amy would have to go to him. *And how do I tell him it's Will I'll be spending spring break with if I go?*

"Is everything OK?" Lou looked up from the pile of receipts she was stapling to invoices.

"I need to talk to you all about who was on the phone," Amy told her.

"Sounds serious." Jack got up from his favorite chair to join the conversation.

Amy nodded. "It's literally a matter of life and death. A horse is so freaked out by an accident he had that if he isn't helped quickly he's going to be put down."

"That *is* serious." Lou narrowed her eyes as she looked at Amy. "The horse must be very unsafe if his owners want to destroy him."

Amy might have known that her sister would take a practical approach to the problem. Quickly she described the details of the accident as Will had told it to her.

"Poor Loup," Lou said softly. She reached across the table to take Amy's hand. "I understand why you want to help, but it shouldn't be at the risk of your own safety."

"What do you think, Ty?" Amy hadn't met his eyes since she'd explained who had made the call. Now that she did, she saw he was obviously surprised she hadn't told him right away that it was Will.

"It sounds like a pretty tough case to me," Ty replied evenly. "But I don't mind if the ranch owner wants to send Loup here, especially with Harlequin and Heart's Ease about to go home."

Amy shifted uncomfortably. "Will wasn't suggesting that they send Loup to us. I think trying to heal him is more Will's idea than the ranch owner's." She looked down and studied her fingernails. "Will's asked me to fly out to Arizona to work with Loup there."

Neither Ty, Lou, nor Jack spoke until Amy glanced back up. Her grandpa was the first to react. "Is this what you want, hon? I don't think you should feel pressured into giving up your time at home."

"It won't be the whole time. I'll come back on Tuesday and have a little time before I have to head back. My first class isn't until Thursday."

"And what about working with Scott?" Lou said.

Amy thought carefully before she replied. She'd enjoyed the first set of rounds with Scott and was looking forward to the rest of her week with him. *But going to Arizona and being based on a cattle ranch would give me a totally new type of experience.* The last thing she wanted to do was disappoint Scott. Would he understand her need to help Loup?

"I think you should go. And I bet that when you check with Scott, he'll say the same," Ty said unexpectedly.

Although Amy was relieved that he was supporting her decision to leave, she was a little hurt that he didn't seem more reluctant to have her go.

"Staying on a cattle ranch will be a great experience," Ty went on. "And I know you. You'll never be able to relax here while you're wondering if you could have done something to help."

Amy gazed into his green eyes and tried to smile. *He could at least tell me he'll miss me if he's not going to convince me to stay. I guess I'm not the only one who thinks things haven't been the same between us since I got back.* Another thought struck her. *What if he's relieved I'm going?*

She checked her watch. "I start work with Scott in a half hour. I'll talk with him then." There would be so much to arrange before she left. She'd have to find a flight, speak to the ranch owner to make sure going out there for the rest of the week would be OK, apply to transfer her internship credit to the vet that Will was shadowing in Arizona, pack, and say good-bye to everyone in just a few hours! She didn't want to waste any time before starting her work with Loup.

"For what it's worth, I think it will be an amazing opportunity," agreed Jack, "as long as you're not allowing your heart to rule your head. As much as Loup's story is a tragic one, he's not your responsibility."

"I know," Amy admitted. "But when you hear a good horse is about to get destroyed and you might be able to save it . . ."

"You've got to try," Ty finished the sentence for her.

"Right." Amy nodded. "But it's important to me that my going is OK with all of you." She looked at Ty as she said it.

"Go get 'em." He half smiled. "Just don't forget us while you're there."

"Never!" Amy said more seriously than she'd intended. "I'll be thinking of Heartland the whole time." She pushed her chair back from the table. "I guess I'd better go see Sunny and Spindle to tell them the news, huh?"

"Just don't let them talk you out of anything," Jack joked.

But as Amy headed down to the paddock, she knew that even if her beloved horses could talk, she wouldn't be persuaded out of taking a chance to help the endangered quarterhorse in Arizona.

℞

Spindle was standing with Heart's Ease but as soon as he saw Amy he left the Appaloosa and trotted over.

"I'm leaving again." Amy reached up to scratch the young horse's temple. Spindle closed his eyes as her fingers worked gently on his skin. "The next time I come back you'll be getting used to a rider. I'll be able to sit on your back for the first time." Spindle nuzzled her shoulder and pretended to chew her hair. Amy hugged him, laughing aloud when he snorted and ran back a few strides. Spindle wheeled around and galloped back to

Heart's Ease who threw his head up as the lively gelding skidded to a halt alongside him.

It was wonderful to see the transformation from the pitiful animal Spindle had been when he first arrived at Heartland to the confident healthy horse in front of her now. *It all comes back to you, Mom, and the work you started here,* Amy thought.

Amy stared over the treetops to the mountains beyond. If her mother hadn't grasped opportunities as they came by, then Heartland wouldn't exist. *I have to do the same.* And even if she didn't know what lay beyond the horizon, at least she'd know that she'd taken the chance to make something wonderful happen.

Scott's Jeep pulled into the yard as Amy was making her way back to the house.

"All ready?" he called out of his open window.

"Do you have a minute before we leave?" Amy asked. "There's something I need to tell you."

Scott glanced at his watch as he got out of the pickup. "We're due at Twin Oaks Farm in a half hour to check on a horse. I guess we can afford a few minutes before going. Don't tell me you've decided to quit because I didn't give you enough exciting cases on your first day?" He winked to show he was teasing.

Amy's cheeks colored. How was she going to convince

Scott that she wasn't snubbing him by leaving? She took a deep breath before telling him about her conversation with Will.

Scott immediately became serious. "Of course you have to go. If you think for one moment you can save Loup from being destroyed, then it's important for you to try. As vets, we're in the business of saving animals' lives."

Amy felt a thrill at being included among the others in Scott's profession even though she had years of hard training ahead of her before she would be a qualified vet. "Apparently that's what Stan, the vet Will is working with, said when he managed to persuade the ranch manager into postponing putting Loup down."

"If you give me his number, I'll give him a call to arrange officially handing you over," Scott suggested. "And maybe you should think about staying home this morning. You've probably got a lot to do to get ready to fly out."

Amy was disappointed at the thought of not going out with him one more time, but could see that his suggestion made sense. "I'll start looking for a cheap flight online," she said. "Thanks, Scott."

"Sure thing," he said, getting back into his Jeep. "Apart from helping Loup, I think that Arizona will be an amazing place for you to be."

Amy nodded, glad that Scott was fine about her leaving,

although she was a little hurt that everyone was OK with her leaving so soon. She told herself she was being overly sensitive. *Heartland will always be my home.*

▬

"So this has nothing to do with the fact that Will is going to be there?" Soraya didn't waste any time getting right to the point when Amy called her.

"Of course not!" Amy denied. She was looking forward to seeing Will, but the only thing that could have convinced her to leave Heartland that week was a horse in crisis.

"Just checking," Soraya told her. "And Ty doesn't have a problem with you going?"

"No," Amy replied. Deep down she wished she could say that Ty was a little jealous, but so far her boyfriend hadn't done anything to show that it was a problem for him.

"It just shows how much he trusts you, I guess," Soraya said. "I'm not sure Anthony would be so cool if I was leaving him to be with Matt."

"But there's never been anything between Will and me," Amy pointed out.

"But Will was interested in you at one point," Soraya reminded her. Then she sighed. "Oh, well. I guess I'll just have to amuse myself for the rest of the week while my best friend's away."

"Nice try." Amy smiled. "Except that you've already told me that Anthony's arriving the day after tomorrow."

"It will be cool having him here and introducing him to everyone — except you, that is! Send me a text message when you get there and let me know how Loup is, OK?" Soraya begged. "And try to find some time when you're not healing horses to have a little fun."

"I will," Amy promised. "I'll call as soon as I get back so you can tell me all about Anthony's visit. You guys have fun, too."

As soon as she hung up, she called Will's cell phone.

"Hey, Amy. Is it OK for you to come out?" He sounded like he expected her to have been convinced not to come.

"Definitely! I've found a flight that arrives in Tucson at three P.M. tomorrow. Is there a bus that runs out to the ranch from the airport?" she asked.

"Leave it to me, I'll find you a ride," Will promised. "I spoke to Hank, the ranch owner, and he said it's fine for you to come and help out with the cattle drive at the end of the week. He wasn't thrilled about you taking a look at Loup but when I mentioned Heartland he finally agreed. Apparently he read an article a while back about the work you do and was pretty impressed. And I couldn't pick anyone I'd rather have to spend time with over here," he said quickly. "I'll see you tomorrow."

"See you," Amy echoed before hanging up.

Amy glanced around at all the photographs lining the walls of her sister's study. Her eye was drawn to the most recent one of her and Ty. Lou had taken a shot of them riding out on Attitude and Fanfare, two of the horses Amy had worked with last summer. She stood up from the desk and went to take a closer look. It had been taken just after Ty had given her the Claddagh ring. They were riding so close that their stirrups were touching, and Lou had caught them just as their eyes had met. Amy blushed, even though there was no one around. It wasn't hard to see how smitten they were with each other. If only Ty could come out with her to Arizona, things would be perfect, but she knew that was impossible. There was no way he could leave Heartland.

Amy reached out and traced her finger over the photo of Ty's face. She was determined to spend as much time as possible with her boyfriend before she left. *We can start with the ride that Ty suggested.* She was suddenly desperate to reestablish their old easy relationship before leaving for Arizona. She couldn't put her finger on what had changed, but she knew there was a distance between them that hadn't been there before.

Chapter Seven

Amy found Ty piecing together a bridle in the tack room. "How about that ride now?"

Ty looked up. "I thought you'd never ask," he joked. "I brought Harlequin and Tarren in earlier but was just about to put them back out."

"When we could be cantering them over Clairdale Ridge? Why would you do that?" Amy grinned.

"I have absolutely no idea," Ty said, playing along and acting as if Amy hadn't been locked away in Lou's study for the past couple of hours. He stood up to take Harlequin's tack off its rack on the wall. "Here you go."

Amy admired the brand-new English leather saddle and bridle. Harlequin's owner didn't seem to spare any expense as far as her horse was concerned. She took the tack down to the gelding's stable and opened the door. "Hey, boy. How about stretching those legs?"

Harlequin nickered softly.

"I'll take that as a yes." Amy smiled. When she picked up the body brush and began working it over his coat, the gelding gave a sigh and half closed his eyes.

"Don't get too laid back, please," Amy told him. "You're going to need to go full throttle to get to the top of Teak's Hill!"

Harlequin's mane was the same colors as his black-and-white coat. Amy combed both his mane and tail until the hair cascaded softly through her hands.

"I bet your owner can't wait to have you back," she said, taking the hoof pick out of the grooming box. Harlequin calmly picked up each foot for her and when she moved around to his front hooves, he dropped his head to nibble at her T-shirt.

"Hey, quit sliming me!" Amy laughed.

Harlequin only stopped at the sound of another horse clopping up the aisle. Ty halted Tarren and looked over the wall. "Are you going to be long?"

"Sorry." Amy straightened up. "I got carried away with the grooming. He's got such gorgeous markings."

"I'll meet you out in the yard," Ty told her. "Tarren hates standing still."

As if he was agreeing with him, the Irish sport horse began to paw the ground.

"I'll be out in two minutes," Amy promised, reaching for Harlequin's bridle.

When she got there, Ty was walking Tarren in circles.

Amy pulled down Harlequin's stirrups so she could mount. "Steady, Harley," she warned as the gelding began to dance on the spot.

"He's livened up," Ty remarked. "It's definitely time for him to go back to his owners. He'll be flying around the next cross-country course he tackles."

"He feels amazing," Amy said enthusiastically as they walked off the yard. Harlequin's stride was long and he covered the ground easily.

Tarren's stride matched Harlequin's and they were able to ride side by side as they made their way up Teak's Hill. Amy couldn't wait to reach the top where the surrounding landscape could be seen stretching out for miles.

She took in a deep breath of the crisp fresh air and felt contentment wash over her. She tried not to think of the fact that this was her last day with Ty until she got back and concentrated instead on how good it felt to be with him.

Ty spoke as if he had heard her thoughts. "I wish this wasn't the last time we were riding out together before you leave."

Relief washed over Amy. How could she have thought Ty wasn't concerned that she was leaving? "I was beginning to think you were totally OK with me leaving." She made her tone light-hearted so Ty wouldn't think she was trying to start a fight.

"You know how much I miss you when you're gone," he told her. "But I understand how important it is for you to go. The day you left for college, I had to accept that your life would be heading in a whole new direction. The only way I can support you is by letting you take every opportunity you can."

"Yes, but that doesn't mean that Heartland isn't my number one priority," Amy objected. She felt stung by Ty's words, even though she knew he was only trying to put her needs first.

"I hate to point this out to you, but you're leaving for Arizona in the morning," Ty said gently. "Maybe you should try to accept that Heartland can't always be your highest priority while you're training to be a vet."

Amy was about to argue with him when Harlequin suddenly half-reared and sprang into a canter. "Steady," she soothed, shortening her reins. She brought the paint horse down to a trot and then a walk before halting for Ty to catch up. This ride was about trying to recapture her old relationship with Ty and disagreeing with him wasn't going to help.

"I think a hornet spooked him," Ty explained. "It buzzed around Tarren after you took off."

Amy leaned forward to stroke Harlequin's neck. "No wonder you didn't want to hang around."

They finished climbing the rest of the hill in silence but when they reached the peak, Ty halted and looked at Amy. "I'm sorry if I upset you when I said Heartland couldn't be your top priority when you're studying."

"That's OK." Amy was relieved that he was taking it back.

"But it's totally understandable that your career is your focus now. You have an amazing talent and the best way to use it is to develop it all the way. Your mom would have understood that and totally supported you. I'm just trying my best to do what I know she would have done."

Amy was at a loss for words as she stared out over the countryside, reminding herself that tomorrow instead of lush greens she'd be seeing the Arizona desert. She was touched by Ty's support, but at the same time she felt frustrated that he didn't fully understand her.

Tarren pawed at the ground, eager to get going again. Ty shortened his reins. "Do you feel like galloping?"

Amy checked her girth. It had slackened enough to go up another two holes. She tightened it and then nodded at Ty. "Ready."

She only had to touch Harlequin's sides for the horse to spring into a fast canter. Amy lifted her weight forward and the canter became a gallop, until the ground and surrounding trees became a blur.

She was aware of Ty and Tarren beside them, matching

Harlequin's every stride. "Go, boy," she urged. Inch by inch, Harlequin edged ahead of the Irish sport horse.

"No fair!" Ty's shout hung on the air for a second and was then snatched away by the breeze and the sound of drumming hooves.

"Last one to the lightning tree has to muck out tonight," Amy yelled over her shoulder.

By the time Harlequin reached the forked tree, Tarren was just a stride behind.

"That was fun." Ty grinned as they gave the horses a loose rein. "Aren't they both amazing?"

"You and Joni have done a great job with them," Amy told him. She patted Harlequin's damp neck.

"And Bunny's recovering quickly, so she should be ready to leave in a couple of days. We'll be almost empty by the end of the week, which is a good thing, I guess, since I took two calls today."

"Yeah?" Amy sat as still as possible to balance Harlequin as he began to pick his way down a pebbled slope.

"One is a Dutch Warmblood who's refusing to be broken in. Apparently he had a bad experience with the first trainer he went to and now he won't let anyone near him. His owner's hoping that our methods might help with a breakthrough."

Amy nodded. "And the other one?"

"A Thoroughbred who's good in every way except for having her feet touched. The owner picked her up at an auction and thought he had a bargain until he went to pick out the horse's hooves. Apparently she went wild and kicked her way out of the stall. They've managed to get the mare shod by sedating her, but obviously they need her to be cured."

"They'll both need Aspen to start to help them deal with fear, Gentian for any discouragement after a setback, and Larch to build confidence," Amy mused, automatically running through the appropriate Bach Flower Remedies. She felt a sense of sadness that she wouldn't be involved in the treatment of either animal. Ty was wrong; Heartland would *always* be her main focus. *But I have to grasp every new experience that comes my way, so I'll end up being the best I can be — for Heartland.*

When they arrived back home, they hosed down the horses. Amy was thrilled to see the way Tarren stood quietly even though the water was running over her hooves.

Harlequin turned to nose at the stream of water, so Amy gently aimed it at his mouth. Harlequin pulled back his lips so she could play the water over his teeth and gums.

"How unusual for a *boy* to enjoy a good bath," Amy joked.

"Hey, I scrub behind my ears and the back of my neck every day, I'll have you know," Ty said, rising to the bait.

"Really?" Amy turned around and raised her eyebrows.

"Amy," Ty said warningly as he stopped slicking water off Tarren's coat with the sweat scraper and backed away holding his hands up in the air.

"You should have stayed close to Tarren," Amy laughed. "I couldn't have done this if you'd been near her."

She closed her finger over part of the opening on the hose, turning the water into a spray, which she directed over Ty. As the water drenched him, Ty tried in vain to find shelter in a corner. Amy laughed playfully as the spray from the hose soaked him despite his efforts to deflect the stream with his hands. Finally, she moved her thumb away and let Ty stand up straight again.

"Right." Ty pushed his wet hair off his face and advanced on Amy.

She sprayed him once more and then dropped the hose. "Sorry!" she squealed as he made a grab for her. Ty spun Amy around and pinned her arms close to her sides. Just as he bent his head toward her, Jack's voice called from the kitchen door.

"Will's on the phone for you, Amy — something about confirming a ride for you from the airport tomorrow."

Ty released her. A muscle twitched in his cheek. "I'll finish up here."

"OK." Amy bit her lip in annoyance. Just as she and

Ty had been getting somewhere, they had to get interrupted. "Grandpa's having a barbecue later since it's my last day. Can you stay for it?"

Ty smiled. "Sure."

❧

Amy held out her plate to Jack for a freshly grilled burger. "That smells terrific," she said appreciatively.

"You'll probably be sick of ranch-style food by the end of the week," he teased.

"Even for breakfast," Nancy said, agreeing with a smile. "Your grandpa's so convinced of it he's been baking muffins for you to take so you don't have to OD on sausages and grits!"

Amy looked around at her family and told herself that she'd hold on to tonight's memory to keep her going while she was in Arizona. She noticed that Lou had her hand on her stomach and looked thoughtful.

"Are you OK?" Amy asked, putting her plate down on the picnic table and hurrying over.

"More Braxton Hicks, hon?" Scott asked.

Lou nodded. "These are just pretend contractions. They're pretty common," she explained to Amy.

Amy went back to sit alongside Ty, who poured her a glass of soda.

"So, are you all packed?" he asked.

Amy nodded. "Nothing but boots, jeans, and T-shirts. I'll be a regular cowgirl."

Ty looked at her through narrowed eyes. "Hmm. Not quite yet. But I think I might be able to help out with that one." He handed Amy a round box.

Mystified, Amy untied the ribbon and lifted off a layer of tissue paper. She pulled out a suede cowboy hat. "Ty! I love it!" Amy cried as she ran her hand over the soft fawn-colored material. "It's gorgeous."

"Here." Ty took it and placed it on her head.

"When did you get it?"

"I made a little detour when I went out to the feed store this afternoon," Ty admitted.

Amy leaned over to hug him. "Thanks, Ty."

Lou nudged Scott. "We've got something for you, too."

"We sure do." Scott pulled out a long cylindrical canvas bag from under his chair. "It's a bedroll to save your delicate bones from nights on hard bunks."

"And the damp ground when you go on the cattle drive," Lou added.

Amy felt her throat ache at the thought of leaving them all. But even though her heart said "stay," her head said loud and clear that going to Arizona was the right thing to do.

Lou yawned. "I think I might have to call it a night. I've got no staying power these days."

"I think an early night would be a good idea for us all. Amy and I have an early start in the morning," Jack said. He would be taking her to the airport the next day.

Ty jumped to his feet. "I've got an early start, too. Stop down at the barn to say good-bye before you leave tomorrow." He dropped a kiss on her forehead and waved good night to everyone else.

Amy stared at his back. *Is that it?* She'd been expecting a few minutes alone with him this evening so they could say their good-byes properly. *Ty makes it sound like he'll fit me in on his way from the stables to the muck pile!*

Struggling not to show her disappointment, she picked up a stack of plates to carry into the kitchen. Just when she thought things were back to normal between Ty and her, he'd thrown her a curveball.

❧

Jack took Amy's bag from her and pretended to buckle under the weight. "I'll put this in the Jeep while you go say good-bye to Ty," he said with a chuckle.

"Thanks, Grandpa."

Amy found Ty washing out buckets just outside the barn. "You're off?" he asked, turning off the tap.

"Yeah, Grandpa's just getting the Jeep out."

"Well, you shouldn't keep him waiting, I guess." Ty walked over to hug her. "I hope everything goes well for you out there and you manage to save Loup. He's definitely got the best possible chance with you being there."

"Thanks." Again, Amy wished Ty would show a little emotion that their week together had been cut so short. Even though she'd been stressed out by his jealousy of Will at the start of the week, she thought it would be nice to see a touch of the green-eyed monster now.

"Well, I guess I'd better get going then," she said.

"Call me when you can to let me know how things are," he told her. "I'll see you Tuesday."

Amy took a deep breath. She had to put aside Ty's reaction so she could give one hundred percent of herself to her work in Arizona. She felt a thrill when she thought that this afternoon she would be experiencing a whole new world. She could deal with her relationship with Ty when she came back. Right now, it was Loup who needed her.

Chapter Eight

"Are you OK, sweetheart? You haven't spoken a word for the last ten miles."

"I was just thinking of everything that's waiting for me in Arizona," Amy admitted.

"Are you thinking that maybe you've taken on a little too much?" Grandpa sounded concerned.

"More that it's difficult to think of everything I'm leaving behind," Amy told him.

"If things get too much out there just remember you'll be home soon," Jack reassured her.

"I guess that's why I can handle new experiences, because I know I always have Heartland and my family," Amy mused.

She knew deep down that Ty hadn't been rejecting her earlier. It was just that, as far as he was concerned, he'd always be there waiting for her, so it wasn't a big deal that she was going away for a few days. Amy felt a surge of love for her boyfriend and wished she'd made more of an effort that morning. He had actually been pretty amazing not to get upset about her going. That was so typical of Ty, putting everyone before himself. Amy resolved to try a little harder from now on to do the same.

"Amy!" Will shouted her name as she made her way out of the airport terminal with her bags.

"Hi!" Amy waved as Will threaded his way through the crowd. He looked very much at home in his dirty jeans and faded plaid shirt. No one would think he was anything but a genuine cowboy.

Will gave her a quick hug. "It's so great you made it."

"It's a lot warmer here than back home." Amy twisted her hair up off her neck, enjoying the sun's rays beating down on her. At night, she knew the desert would be cool, but even though it was still early spring, the day was pleasantly warm. "Cool car," she added, admiring the beat-up, sand-colored four-wheel-drive vehicle.

"Hank let me borrow one of the ranch Jeeps," Will explained as they both slid onto the front seat.

"He sounds pretty laid back," Amy commented.

"He is," Will agreed. "But when it comes to work

around the ranch he takes things seriously. He's quick to crack the whip if he thinks anyone's not pulling their weight."

Amy didn't have a problem with that. She understood what it took to run a place with lots of animals and people. "What's the latest on Loup?" she asked.

"I did what you suggested last night and spent time with him while still giving him space. He was restless at first — he probably thought I was going to try to ride him. But once he realized I wasn't a threat, he let me feed him some treats and stroke his neck." He sighed. "It's so hard seeing the change in him since he was ridden. He seemed totally recovered from the attack and was really friendly to everyone. After he threw Sam, he turned into a totally different animal. I was thinking it must be a psychophysiological disorder like in that case study we were looking at earlier this year. Loup's symptoms are coming from a mental problem rather than immediate physiological causes."

Amy nodded. "That's what I think, too. He had to confront his fear of having a rider on his back, and it sounds as if he regressed to the day of the attack. I think it's more than losing all trust in the person who rides him. . . ."

"He sees any rider as a threat," Will ended for her.

Amy nodded, admiring the way Will was combining his medical knowledge with his natural intuitiveness.

"So, what will you do to restore his trust in riders?" Will asked.

"I'm going to try a couple of techniques on Loup that we use at Heartland," Amy replied. "They're used to build or renew trust between a horse and its handler."

She rolled down the window and enjoyed the wind streaming in. "Have you managed to get through any reading for school?"

Will laughed. "If you want to get any reading done while you're on the ranch, then between midnight and five in the morning is about the only time to do it," Will told her. "Enjoy your last twenty minutes of quiet. Very soon the ride's going to get B-U-M-P-Y," he spelled out.

"I hope you're not speaking literally," Amy teased with a glance at the road. No matter how hard the work on the ranch was she couldn't wait to get started.

They had long ago left the city behind, and the landscape was breathtaking. They'd passed a towering forest and then lush flowering grassland but were now driving through more barren terrain. Rocky mountain ranges dominated miles of land that looked as if it hadn't seen a drop of water in years. The grass was gray, a strange contrast to the beautiful greens they'd driven by earlier. Amy leaned out of the window as a brown bird of prey descended from the skies to settle on a huge cactus.

"A Harris hawk," Will told her, pointing out the bird. "The wildlife here is amazing."

"What have you seen so far?" Amy asked. "Apart from cattle!"

"I got a glimpse of a horned toad a couple of days ago," Will said excitedly. "And Max, who's in the bed next to mine, swears he saw a tarantula disappearing under the porch."

"I'm beginning to wish I didn't ask!"

The dusty road leading off from the main highway was in a state of disrepair. "Don't worry, it's only five miles long," Will said after one particularly hard jolt.

"Are you serious?" Amy groaned.

"I'm afraid so," Will declared.

But the bad section soon gave way to a smoother surface, and Amy heaved a sigh of relief.

Shallow Creek Ranch was much bigger than Amy had imagined. The main house, which was low-roofed with a long porch running its length, was at the center of the other ranch buildings. Beyond the log cabins and bunkhouses, the barns and corrals were full of cattle.

Two German shepherds jumped down off the front porch of the ranch house and ran toward the Jeep, barking.

"That's where they keep the horses." Will pointed to a huge group of stalls. "The rest are in the barn out back."

"It must take a lot of people to run this place," Amy said, thinking how small Heartland seemed by comparison.

"There's Hank," Will added, stopping the Jeep near one of the corrals. He nodded at a deeply tanned man who was stretching wire around posts to secure some old fencing. "Come say hi. He breeds his own horses in addition to working with the cattle. You'll probably find you've got lots of stuff in common."

Amy hopped out of the Jeep and walked over with Will to meet Hank.

"Be with you in a minute," the ranch owner mumbled because of the three nails he had pressed between his lips. "Pass that hammer, will you?"

Will picked up the hammer by Hank's feet and handed it to him. Hank drove in the nails with ease and then stood back to look over the corral fencing. He grunted and wiped his hand on a rag before turning to Amy. "Will's college friend here to work for the rest of the week, right?"

Amy nodded. "Thanks for letting me come out." She had to raise her voice over the bellowing of the cattle.

Hank gave a short laugh. "See if you thank me at the end of the week after you've got through your work quota!" He winked at Will.

"I'm looking forward to seeing what I can do with Loup," Amy said.

Hank took off his wide-brimmed hat and ran his hand through his short blond hair. "Will had to do a lot of talking before I agreed to let you look at that animal. Looking at you, I'm even less convinced that it's a good idea. If he threw one of my two-hundred-pound ranch hands, what's he going to do to a lightweight like you? He's dangerous and that means he hasn't got any place on a working ranch."

Amy felt taken aback by his bluntness. "I've worked with lots of horses just like Loup. . . ."

"I know, I read about your work," Hank interrupted. "It's the only reason I said yes to you coming out here." He sighed. "You work horses off the ground to start with, right?"

Amy nodded. "It's called join-up."

Hank waved his hand. "I don't care what name it's known by. I just care if you get the results." He paused. "I'll let you work with Loup around your work and ranch chores, but if you want to try and ride him I want it checked through me. Deal?"

Amy stuck out her hand. "Deal." She was tempted to spit on her hand before shaking just to see his reaction.

Almost as if he'd read her thoughts, Hank's blue eyes twinkled as he shook her hand. He turned to Will. "You'd better take Amy to the bunkhouse for her to drop off her stuff and then I suppose you'll want to show her that crazy horse before supper."

Will nodded. "Sure."

"I don't think there's a chance of breaking through to Loup before the end of the week," Hank added. "But I sure as hell hope it happens. He was the best horse on this ranch. When he was rounding up cattle he knew which way to turn before his rider did. It would be a real shame to have to destroy him."

Amy opened her mouth to respond but Hank already had his back to her and was heading off toward the house.

She stared after him, feeling more determined than ever to help the troubled quarterhorse. *I'll do everything I can to save him, I promise.*

Amy and Will walked past more corrals all of which had cattle milling around in them. The air was thick with the red dust kicked up by hundreds of hooves.

"They've just about all been rounded up from their winter pasture surrounding the ranch. We're going to spend the next few days checking them over, branding the new cows, worming, vaccinating, and hoof trimming before we drive them out to their summer grazing," Will explained. "Stan — the vet that I'm working with — will be spending a couple of hours on site each day, which means we get to do a lot of our work with him here."

"It sounds great," Amy replied.

The bunkhouses were behind the main house. "This is the girls'," Will said, walking up the two steps onto the veranda. "The two bunks closest to the door are free, so take whichever one you want."

Amy pushed open the door and stepped into a small hallway cluttered with rain gear, hats, and boots. A door on her right opened on to the sleeping quarters where bunks lined both sides of the room. Most of the beds had sleeping bags rolled up on them except for the two Will had mentioned. She threw her backpack, sleeping bag, and bedroll on top of the nearest empty bunk. Then she placed the container of herbal remedies she'd brought with her in the bedside cabinet and headed back outside.

Will was waiting for her on the veranda. "I know it must have been a sacrifice leaving home, but it's not all bad, is it?" He waved his hand at the surrounding mountains.

Amy didn't reply immediately. It was hard to find the words to respond to the breathtaking scenery that stretched for miles into the distance. The sky looked as if it was on fire, engulfed with orange-and-red flames as the sun dipped behind the majestic craggy mountains. It was a raw, wild beauty that looked as if it had been there forever and would go on forever. A purple haze shimmered over the distant ground making her feel as if she had stumbled into an enchanted land. She smiled at the thought.

"Do you want to go see Loup?" Will asked.

Amy nodded. She couldn't wait to see the animal who was at one with these surroundings; an animal who had survived an attack by a mountain lion and had come back fighting. He had to be an amazing horse. She wasn't going to let Hank give up without trying everything she could to help him.

Chapter Nine

There were three horses looking out over the row of stalls. Amy knew instinctively which was Loup. He wasn't the gray looking at them with his ears pricked with interest. Nor was he the bay dozing in the last of the sunlight hitting the stalls. He was the palomino with the oversized head, who warily watched them approach. She could tell from the expression in his eyes — an expression that said he hadn't known peace in a long while. As if to confirm her guess, the gelding flinched at a distant gunshot and disappeared into the darkness of his stall.

"He doesn't like to hear shots. Even from a distance," Will muttered as he pulled the bolt open on the door. He flicked on the light switch.

Amy took in a sharp breath when she saw the long

scars on Loup's flank and quarters. The wounds had been deep and jagged, each one reflecting the sharp, knifelike claws of the mountain lion. Her stomach turned as she pictured the horse being attacked, being robbed of his peace of mind, of his trust in humans, of his unity with his place of birth. "Poor, poor, boy," she whispered.

His golden coat was dull with dried patches of sweat and even as Amy stared, Loup began to perspire. "He should have a blanket on to keep him from getting a chill," she murmured.

"I'm on it," Will said, reaching for both the anti-sweat blanket and stable rug that were hitched on a line out of Loup's reach on the back wall of the stall.

Amy stared at Loup's face with its slight Roman nose and noticed the honest, wide-set eyes that indicated a sharp intelligence. The shape of his head implied a stubborn, proud character. A single whorl on his forehead suggested a single-minded, focused nature that had once been seen in his dedication to his handlers and had since been transferred to his fear of being ridden.

The personality traits shown in his face gave Amy hope that he might begin to respond to her treatment before she would have to leave. The single-mindedness that made him focused in his distrust could possibly make him centered on his healing. *But will it be enough to save him from being put down? He's got a long way to go and he's not going to cover the whole distance in the four days I'm here.*

Watching Will buckle the rug on, Amy began mentally listing the remedies she would use to help Loup deal with the trauma of his accident. She would give him some Fenugreek to help stimulate his appetite since his hay net hadn't been touched. *And a spritzer would be good; something immediate to spray into the air.* She would have loved to go back to her bags in the bunkhouse and begin preparing Loup's remedies from the selection of bottles she had brought with her, but Will had already told her that there wasn't time to do anything other than look Loup over before going for supper.

"I'll be back right after dinner to give you something that will make you start to feel better," she told the gelding. She wished she had Joni's skill with acupuncture to aid Loup's recovery. *Maybe it's something I should think about studying sometime in the future.* She smiled at the thought. At this rate, she'd never be done with school.

Amy slowly moved over the straw to the back of the stall, holding out her hand to Loup and talking in a soothing voice. "Easy fella, I'm not going to hurt you."

Loup gave a long suspicious snort, and in response Amy dipped her head and blew gently into his nostrils. After a pause, Loup blew back.

"There," Amy murmured. "That's a start." She reached up to scratch his forehead.

"What was that you just did?" Will asked in a quiet voice.

"It's a horsey way of saying hello," Amy told him. "You want to try?"

Will copied exactly what she had done and Loup breathed back at him. "That's amazing," he said, standing up straight. "It's like speaking a different language!"

"There are lots of ways of communicating with horses on their level instead of trying to force them to act in an unnatural way," Amy said. "My horse, Spindle, is being trained using nothing but natural methods and it's great to see the way he's keeping his spunky, confident personality."

"So you wouldn't use the expression 'breaking in' for what you're doing with him?" Will's eyes were bright with interest.

"Nope." Amy shook her head. "We'll ask him to trust us to ride him, not force him to accept us with whips and spurs. It's a way of forming a true partnership with a horse."

"I'm looking forward to you showing all this to me," Will told her. "But right now we'd better go eat. If you don't go for your food when the tin pan outside the cabin is beaten, then you wait until the next meal. Right now, I don't think I can wait until breakfast." He grinned. "So, speaking of being on a horse's level, I'm ready to eat like one!"

❧

It was a short walk over to the dining house, which was similar to the bunkhouses but a little larger.

"I've been sitting at the table over there for the last couple of nights." Will nodded at a trestle table in the middle of the room that already had a number of people sitting at it. "They're a good crowd. They're all studying at Boston University and came out here for a break from the city. Do you want to go sit with them?"

"Sure." Amy would have preferred a quieter meal with just Will on her first night so they could talk more about Loup, but she guessed that mixing with lots of new people was just par for the course on the ranch.

Once they'd served themselves some hamburger casserole and mashed potatoes and walked over to the table, Will handled the introductions in his easy style. "Amy, this is Corey, Max, and Scooby." The three of them smiled at her. "Don't be put off by Corey if he says or does anything strange. He's still in shock that he's surrounded by real live cows and horses. None of us can figure out what he thought he was coming for when he signed up for a cattle drive."

"Oh, come on!" Corey laughed, running his hand over his long sun-streaked hair. "I heard the others say the word 'vacation' and then I tuned out. I didn't know I was going to end up cattle rustling."

"He started to get suspicious when we wouldn't let him bring his surfboard on the plane," Max joked.

"There's no need to act all superior just because you were a cowboy in a previous lifetime," Corey pretended to grumble.

Scooby winked at Amy. "We're all placing bets that Max drops out of college to become a wrangler."

Max stuck out his hand to shake Amy's. "Let's just say that I'm feeling the call of the wild in a major way."

"I think I know how you feel." She smiled.

"And over to the girls," Will said, turning to the two dark-haired students sitting opposite the boys.

"Saving the best until last," the taller of the two quipped.

"Just what I was about to say." Will grinned. "This is Kirsten, here to keep the rest of us in our place."

"Don't you forget it," she said sweetly. "Hi, Amy. It's good to have another girl on board."

"Hi," Amy replied.

"And this is Leila who's into horses almost as much as you and is dying for you to tell her everything you know about alternative remedies," Will finished.

Amy sat down alongside the girls. "Nice to meet you, Leila. Do you have your own horse?"

"A rather feisty Arab called Speedy Gonzales, Gonzo for short." She smiled. "But he's stabled twenty miles away from home so I only get to ride him on the weekends. Someday I plan to have my own place with enough land to keep him with me."

"Don't listen to her," Kirsten joined in. "She's got no intention of keeping Gonzo in a field. He'll be free to roam the house, and she won't bat an eyelash at sharing her cornflakes with him every morning."

"That's a great idea." Amy laughed. "I've only ever gone as far as sleeping in a horse's stall. I'd never thought of bringing them in the house before, although I'm not sure my sister would be OK with it!" She imagined Lou's face at the sight of Sundance standing at the end of the table in the kitchen with his nose in a cereal bowl.

"Does that mean your mom would be cool with it?" Corey asked as he poured himself some water from the jug on the table.

"I don't think even my mom would have put up with having a horse in the house, but she died a while back," Amy replied.

Corey looked stricken. "I'm sorry. Me and my motormouth."

"It's fine, really," Amy said quickly. "I'm OK talking about her. In fact, I guess my mom is really the reason that I'm here. It was because of her that I got interested in helping to heal horses and that led to the pre-veterinary program at Virginia Tech."

"That's right. Will told us that you're here to help cure Loopy Loup," Scooby said.

"There's nothing that's going to fix that horse in just a few days." Max jumped in to the conversation. He broke a bread roll and waved it animatedly as he spoke. "He's not right in the head. Everyone thought he'd recovered from the attack until Sam got on him the other day and Loup practically broke his back. What's to stop him looking as if he's OK after a few days with you and then turning psycho again when you try to get on him?"

"I'm not denying that it's a risk," Amy agreed. "But that's something I've grown used to over the years."

"I'm with Max. I think Loup should have been put down already." Kirsten shot Leila an apologetic look. "Sorry, Lei, I know you're really hoping Amy's going to wave a magic wand."

"It's not magic," Amy said. "It's getting into the horse's mind and trying to work with him from his perspective."

"So," Scooby leaned forward, "tell us Loup's perspective."

Amy swallowed her mouthful of spicy casserole. "Horses are herd animals and their way of feeling secure is by sticking together and fleeing from any danger. They'll nearly always choose flight over fight. Two of the worst things happened for Loup when he was in that canyon. First his rider, his *partner*, abandoned him and left him to face the danger alone. Then, when Loup was trapped in the canyon, his rider came back and shot at the lion. More than likely, Loup thought his rider was aiming at him. It was enough to totally shatter Loup's trust in his rider — or in any rider. He's afraid he's going to be taken out into danger again."

Corey looked impressed. "Whoa, no one told me you were a horse shrink!"

"I'm not!" Amy held her hands up in the air. "It just comes from years of being around horses and watching how they react to things."

"So, what will you use to cure him?" Leila had abandoned her fork and forgotten about her food, she was so wrapped up in what Amy was saying.

"I'll start off by giving him some Bach Flower Remedies tonight," Amy told her.

Corey frowned. "Wasn't he a composer?"

"Not this Bach!" Amy smiled. "An English scientist called Dr. Edward Bach discovered that the essences from different plants can help cure various emotional problems."

One of the wranglers who had been sitting at a nearby table abruptly pushed back his chair and stood over Amy. "What you're planning is a total waste of time. There are seventy horses working here, what's the point in taking a risk on one that's turned loco?" The man's small dark eyes burned with an antagonism that Amy couldn't understand. Before she could reply, the wrangler turned and stomped out of the cabin.

Amy's cheeks burned and she stared down at her casserole, wanting to be anywhere other than where she was right now.

"Mike's kind of sensitive about Loup," Will murmured. "It was his brother, Sam, who rode Loup into the canyon and who tried riding him again this week."

"It was Mike's brother who was thrown?" Amy pressed her hands against her cheeks. "No wonder he reacted like he did. He must have thought I was blaming the whole thing on Sam."

Kirsten smiled sympathetically. "Don't worry about it. We all knew where you were coming from and what you said made a lot of sense."

Amy was grateful for Kirsten's reaction, but she still ate her meal as fast as possible so she could quickly get back out to Loup. At least by working with him she felt close to being on familiar ground. Sometimes it was a lot easier to be around horses than people.

As soon as Amy had collected the bottles she needed, she went down to the stable block. Will was already in with Loup, running his hand gently down the quarter horse's neck. "He feels really tense."

"I've got a few things to help him with that," Amy told

him. She showed Will the small spritzer bottle containing a blend of grapefruit seed extract, lavender, marjoram, vetiver, and orange. "It should have an effect as soon as he breathes it in and that will make him more open to the other remedies we'll use," she explained, spraying the mist into the air.

Immediately, the stall was filled with the warm mellow smell of orange and lavender. "It works on humans, too," Will said, inhaling. "Can I have some to spray in my room back in college when Macintosh gives one of her killer assignments?"

"And give you an unfair advantage? No way," Amy teased.

Loup flinched at the sound of their voices and shifted restlessly in the straw.

He's as tight as a guitar string. Amy reached for the Bach Flower Remedies she'd brought. "I'm giving him Star of Bethlehem for shock, and Sweet Chestnut because there's bound to be underlying depression after the experience he's had." She put a few drops into Loup's water bucket. "There's Larch in there, too, for building up his confidence."

"Wouldn't it be easier to give him a sedative?" Will asked.

Amy shook her head. "That's just temporarily masking the problem. The herbs make him more open to healing, but a sedative would just dull his senses."

"So you would say that conventional medicine's done everything it can do for Loup and basically failed?" Will raised his eyebrows.

"Not failed," Amy said quickly. "Loup's wounds are healing, and he hasn't had any further physical complications thanks to the great care he's received. What conventional medicine can't do is fix the emotional trauma."

"And that's where you come in," Will added. "So, is there anything else you're going to do right now or do we wait for what you've already given him to kick in?"

"There is one other thing I'd like to show you," Amy admitted. "I think Loup will be more relaxed with you doing it because he knows you a lot better than me."

"What is it? Helping him to count sheep? I don't think we'll fit many in here," Will joked.

"Will, your jokes are as awful out here as they are at school." Amy gave him a gentle push. "You're going to do T-touch on Loup. It's like massage for animals and is great for helping them relax."

"There's no table for him to lie on," Will said straight-faced. But, despite the jokes, when he laid his hand on Loup's neck where Amy showed him, he was totally focused.

Loup snorted and sidestepped away. Amy waited for him to quiet before approaching him again. "You need to move your fingers in small circles. Using pressure rotation helps to release energy and relax Loup." She covered Will's hand with hers and helped show him the movement. "A little more pressure . . . perfect."

"He still feels really tight," Will said after a few minutes.

"Remember, nothing's going to happen overnight," Amy said. "But he's definitely looking less tense between the eyes." She drew an invisible line across Loup's forehead. "Are you OK to keep going? If you are, we'll peel back his rugs and work his other side. We can also start massaging lavender oil into his coat now that he trusts us to touch him."

"Sure thing," Will agreed, bending his head close to Loup as he massaged him. The deep red of his hair stood out against the gelding's sandy-colored coat.

They spent the next twenty minutes massaging Loup, and Amy told Will about some of the horses that had been treated over the years with Heartland techniques. "Once I flew out to Australia and worked with a couple of my dad's horses. One of them reminds me of Loup. Every time Mistral was handled, she broke into a sweat and got totally distressed. My dad knew she was a great horse, but just couldn't break through to her!"

"And did you help her before it was time to leave?" Will sounded hopeful.

Amy nodded. "Mistral had some emotional trauma

that needed working out of her system. She was finally beginning to trust again by the time I left."

She stopped moving her fingers against Loup's skin, pleased that at last his muscles felt unknotted. "Good boy," she praised him softly before slipping his blankets back over his back and buckling them.

Loup let out a deep sigh as if he was disappointed they had stopped. "We'll come see you in the morning," Amy promised before following Will out.

"Amy, look!" Will whispered when he turned to switch off the light.

Amy glanced over her shoulder to see Loup reaching out for his hay net and taking a mouthful of hay. "That's great!"

As Will closed the door, a few of the horses in the adjacent stalls moved restlessly. There was a whinny from the far end on the opposite side of the quad.

"What're you guys doing down here?" Mike appeared from the end stall on Loup's row. "The horses need to get their rest. They worked hard today."

"Sorry," Will apologized. "We were just leaving."

Mike followed them off the yard as if he didn't trust them to go. A Jeep pulled up a little ahead of them, and Amy's heart sank when she saw Hank get out. The way Mike was stalking after them made it look like they'd been up to no good.

As they drew closer to the ranch owner, Mike spoke again. "Next time you want some time out together choose somewhere there isn't livestock around. A working ranch isn't the place to be romancing."

Amy took in a sharp breath at Mike's accusation that they had snuck off to be alone.

Will spun around. "Hey, we're just friends, OK?"

"Whatever." Mike shrugged. "Just as long as you haven't come out here to play wranglers instead of really working."

"You think what Amy does is playing?" Will sounded incredulous. "She really started to get through to Loup tonight."

"Will . . ." Amy tried to interrupt but Will was in full defense mode.

"You'll have a lot of apologizing to do when she gets Loup ready for the cattle drive at the end of the week!"

Amy stared at him in horror. There was no way Loup would be ready by then!

Mike snorted. "You get that horse ready by the end of the week, and I'll personally stop the vet from coming with his gun."

As Amy struggled to find the right words to say that Loup's progress wouldn't be that fast, Will stuck out his hand to Mike.

"Deal," he said.

Chapter Ten

Mike shook Will's hand and barked out a laugh. "My brother rode that horse every day for the last six years. They were partners; always knew what the other was thinking. You're telling me that in a few days you can get through to the horse that deliberately broke his back?"

Amy felt shaken. *No wonder Loup reacted this badly. It wasn't just any rider who abandoned him. It was the person he trusted more than anyone else not to let him down.*

"Can you spare a minute, Mike?" Hank interrupted.

Amy had totally forgotten the ranch owner standing behind them. She waited for Hank and Mike to walk away together before she turned to Will. "I wish you hadn't said that. There's enough pressure already just to get Loup improved by the end of the week without signing him up for a cattle drive."

Will looked apologetic. "I'm sorry. Mike just really wound me up. I guess it was a dumb thing to promise."

Amy sighed. "It doesn't matter. Loup's destiny is in Hank's hands and I'm sure he won't be expecting him to be ready for the cattle drive. I'm just hoping to turn Loup around enough to persuade Hank to give him another chance. After that, the rest of his recovery will have to be taken over by someone else on the ranch while we go home."

Home. She had totally forgotten to call Ty and tell him what was going on with Loup! Amy checked the time and knew that with the time difference between Arizona and Virginia, it would be too late to call now. *I'll call him first thing in the morning.*

When Amy woke in the morning, she got dressed quietly so she wouldn't disturb any of the other girls in the bunkhouse, and then slipped outside. It was five A.M. and the air was crisp and clear. Amy enjoyed having the morning to herself. It gave her a chance to finally breathe and adjust to the fact that she wasn't at college or at Heartland; she was at Shallow Creek Ranch: a whole new place with new possibilities.

The sunrise spilled over the horizon in a pool of gold. As she stood on the porch, Amy listened to the morning chorus of birds competing with the crickets. Despite her worries about Loup, she felt herself relax. Shallow Creek Ranch was the most amazing place.

She dialed Ty's cell and he picked up after three rings.

"Hey, I thought you were having such a good time out there you weren't going to call until you got back to Virginia and needed a ride!"

It seemed like Ty was trying to joke but she thought she could detect an edge to his tone.

"How's everything at home. Is Lou OK?"

"She's fine," Ty reassured her. "If there was any news we wouldn't wait to call you. Everything's pretty quiet around here, to tell you the truth. Heart's Ease and Harlequin are leaving today, and I'm dropping Tarren off tomorrow. How are things with you?"

"It's incredible here. Everyone's been really nice." She hesitated, wondering if she should tell him about Mike's hostility, then decided against it. "I spent some time with Loup last night, massaging him with lavender oil."

"Did you put Bach Flower Remedies into his water?"

"Yes, and sprayed the spritzer we usually use on anxious horses," Amy told him. "You should see him, Ty. He's so withdrawn and tense. I'm sure from the shape of his head that he's a single-minded horse and at the moment he's totally focused on one thing: fear."

"Have you thought about using Mimulus to help with the fright?"

"I'm not sure I packed any," Amy said, "but that's a great idea. I'll check my box of remedies."

"It's a shame you can't give him a while to let the remedies and T-touch really kick in before you start handling him."

"I know," Amy agreed. "But I'm going to have to try to join-up with him later today."

"I'll be thinking of you," Ty said.

"Me, too," Amy said. "Give my love to everyone."

When she hung up she thought how much she appreciated being able to talk things through with Ty. Even if they were out of sync on a personal level right now, their working relationship was still in tune. She knew he was right about not pushing Loup too soon, but she couldn't help feeling an excited buzz at the thought of joining up with the gelding. She'd go see him now and give him another session of T-touch to help put him in the right frame of mind.

Loup was dozing when Amy arrived. He snorted as she stepped into his stall but at least he didn't move away from her. She held out her hand for him to sniff. "Do you remember me? I'm going to be your best friend for the next few days."

She unbuckled the chest straps so she could remove Loup's blanket. His coat had much more of a sheen than when she had first seen it, thanks to the work she and Will had done the night before. "I'll give you a full grooming this afternoon before I take you out," she promised.

She unscrewed the top of the lavender bottle and tipped some oil into her palm. The heady aroma filled the stall as Amy began to work the oil into Loup's coat. She admired the flecks of gold among the sandy hairs beneath her fingers. Loup would never win a prize for best show pony but she bet that out on the prairie, racing after a runaway steer with his tail streaming in the wind, he was a gorgeous sight.

Loup responded more quickly to the massage this time and soon Amy felt him relax against her fingers. "You realize I'm no threat, huh? But will you still think that when I take you out of your stable later?"

She decided to leave Loup's blanket off since he seemed relaxed enough not to be breaking into an anxious sweat. She left his stall and refreshed his water pail, adding the rescue remedies to the bucket again.

"I'll be back later," she told him.

Loup looked at her steadily, and Amy wondered what he was thinking. Did he sense she wanted to help him? Amy's fingers tightened into her palms. Loup *had* to respond to the join-up, it was the first step for him to regain his trust in people. But she knew it was a lot to ask of him so soon. *Too soon.*

Will was already eating when Amy made it to the cabin. She helped herself to orange juice, eggs, and bacon. Grandpa had been right about there being a lot of meat on the menu. There had to be room for a hundred sausages on the hot plate!

"Hey, where've you been? I thought you were going to miss breakfast," Will asked. "Did you sleep OK?" Only he and Max were left at the table. The hall was emptying rapidly as everyone went to get started on their ranch work.

"Good, thanks," Amy replied. "I woke up early so I put some time in with Loup."

Max pushed the ketchup over. "What did you do?"

"Horse massage," Amy told him. "I'm hoping to take him out to a corral this afternoon and work him from the ground."

"Cool," Max replied. "I'd love to come watch but I promised Scooby and Corey that I'd go see their first try at loping."

"Before anyone staying here can come out on the cattle drive they have to prove they can walk, trot, lope, stop, and turn," Will explained. "Some of the wranglers give lessons in the afternoons for anyone who needs to brush up on their riding skills."

"I can't wait to see Scooby tackling barrels at a lope," Max said, his dark eyes mischievous.

Amy shot a grin at Will. "What's our schedule for today? Can we fit in a look at Scooby's lesson?"

"Unlikely," Will replied. "We're meeting with Stan in," he checked his watch, "fifteen minutes. We'll be spending the morning with him, breaking for lunch, then we have to help brand the new calves and, after that, we'll be able to work with Loup."

Amy dug into her breakfast, understanding why the ranch hands all had a big meal to kick off the day. No matter how much she loved Jack's muffins, they wouldn't give her the energy she needed to tackle everything that lay in front of her.

Clearing her plate, she drained the last of her juice. "See you at lunch, Max."

"Have a good morning," he called after them.

Amy and Will made their way over to the ranch house where Stan's green truck was parked. The vet was counting through wrapped medication packages in the back.

"Reporting for duty, Stan." Will made a mock salute.

Stan stopped what he was doing and turned to greet them. "It's good to have you on board, Amy." He shook her hand. "We've got quite a bit to get to this morning."

"Are we staying here on the ranch?" Will asked.

Stan nodded. "One of the steers was kicked and his leg needs looking at. All the cattle in the first corral need vaccinating, and Hank's asked us to look at one of his horses." He zipped up his bag and covered up his receding hairline with a baseball cap. "Let's go look at this steer."

One of the ranch hands was waiting for them by a holding cage with smooth clamps on either side keeping the animal still.

"It's his right hind leg," the wrangler told Stan.

"Thanks, Joe." Stan set down his bag.

On the steer's back leg was a long deep gash. Amy winced when she saw it. "Is it going to need stitches?" she asked.

"I'll let you two offer your opinions first," Stan told her. He pulled back one of the railed fences for Amy and Will to get near the steer.

Will reached over to run his hand down the cow's hind leg. "There's quite a bit of heat and swelling." The cow gave a bellow of protest and tried to kick out at Will. "Steady." He examined the wound before standing back to give Amy a look.

The skin was inflamed, as Will had said, but the wound wasn't as deep as she had first thought. "I don't think it needs stitching but, judging by the heat and swelling, there could be an infection developing."

"And what's the best course of action for that?" Stan asked, going to check the steer.

"Antibiotics," Amy and Will said together.

Stan crouched down by the steer's right hind leg and examined the wound. "I agree. If the wound was on a different animal, say, a top show pony, then obviously we'd stitch to help it heal as cleanly as possible. In this case when it's a big tough old steer," he slapped the animal's rump, "then there's no call to try to keep him looking pretty."

Stan took Intrasite gel out of his case and applied it to the wound to help keep it clean. "Thanks, Joe. You can let him go now. I'll give you the antibiotics before I leave; they're in the back of the Jeep." He shouldered his bag. "Let's go look at this horse of Hank's."

Hank kept his horses separate from the ranch ponies. They had their own barn and the first two stalls were extra large for foaling. The barn's back doors opened out onto a paddock that was divided into three grazing areas. Amy peered through the doors at the small group of grazing mares and youngsters. She noticed the arched muscular necks, the powerful bodies, and the long sweeping tails. "Wow, Tennessee walking horses." She knew the breed had been created from some of the best in the world, including Thoroughbreds, Morgans, and American Saddlebreds to end up with an incredible show and trail-riding horse. She would have loved to go take a closer look at them but, instead of going outside, Stan stopped at the end stall. A girl about Amy's age was in with the sick mare. Amy immediately noticed the chestnut's flanks were heaving as if she'd just done strenuous exercise.

"Hi, Stan." The stable girl patted the mare's neck before walking over to the door. "I'll go get Hank. He wanted to be here for your examination."

"Thanks, Nicky," Stan said, holding the door open for Will and Amy to go in ahead of him. He got out his stethoscope and handed it to Amy. "Have a listen."

Amy patted the mare's neck and then pressed the metal disk over her flank. There was a faint crackle each time the mare inhaled. Amy handed the stethoscope to Will and moved to the horse's head. She checked her air passages and saw that there was mucus in her nostrils.

Stan raised his eyebrows. "Any suggestions?"

Amy had seen something like this at Heartland, although that had been a far more extreme case. "She sounds like she's got a respiratory infection. I'm wondering if it could be chronic obstructive pulmonary disorder."

"Good analysis." Hank spoke behind them. "Absolutely correct, in fact. Trinket was diagnosed six months ago after a viral infection. I called Stan to come examine her because she's become destabilized and she's going to need medication."

"After we dealt with the initial symptoms, just keeping her outside kept the worst of the disease at bay," Stan told them. "It's going to be medication again, I'm afraid, until her breathing clears."

"Well done," Will murmured as he left the stall with Amy.

"Thanks." She flashed him a smile. "You would have come to the same conclusion." Will smiled back.

"OK." Stan had joined them. "Are you ready to go vaccinate a whole lot of cows?"

Amy took a last look at the grazing horses. There was an incredibly cute yearling that reminded her of Spindle, looking all legs as he skittered around the paddock with an older filly.

"If you have any time off this week then come back up and have a look around," Hank offered.

"Thanks, I'd like that," Amy said.

As they walked down to the corrals with Stan she realized that even if she had a whole month here it wouldn't be long enough to experience every aspect of ranch life. But she was here to help Loup and until the week was through, he would be her total focus.

❧

Amy felt like every bone in her body was aching when she, Stan, and Will finished for the day. The branding had been the most exhilarating but exhausting task. The wranglers had expertly roped the unbranded calves, and Amy and Will had helped hold them down so they could be marked with the ranch's brand.

"Tell me again why we have to do this," Amy asked Will with a pained look. She knew branding was necessary for open-range cattle, but she'd never be completely comfortable with the practice.

"It's the only way to keep straight whose cattle are whose when they're all allowed to roam free. It's better than keeping them cooped up their whole lives."

Amy knew Will was right about the benefit of letting the animals graze freely, so she resolved not to think too much about the momentary pain branding seemed to cause them.

Loup was looking over his door when they approached his stall. "Is it just me, or does he look pleased to see us?" Will asked.

"He certainly doesn't look unhappy," Amy replied, noting Loup's pricked ears and the way he was following them with his eyes.

"So, tell me again what we're going to do with him," Will said.

"We're going to take him down to one of the empty corrals and turn him loose. I'm going to make him run from me with the hope that he'll get sick of running and will want to be my friend instead."

"I still don't see how it can work," Will said, holding

the stall door open for Amy. "I mean, how does a horse ask to be your friend?"

"You'll see," she told him. *At least I hope you'll see.*

They worked some more T-touch on Loup before Amy reached for his halter, which was hanging just outside the door. As soon as she slipped it over his nose, Loup ran backward. Amy was ready for him and followed his movement. She quickly finished buckling the halter on, murmuring to him, "Hold still. There's a clever boy."

Will held the door open for them. "He doesn't look happy."

Amy agreed but didn't have a chance to say anything because the moment they walked out onto the yard Loup pulled strongly against Amy's hold on him and almost knocked her off her feet. *Anything to get away from me.*

Loup jogged all the way down to the corral and Amy had to stop a few times and let him circle her before she could regain control of him. It wasn't a great start. She let Loup go the moment they were in the corral and the gate was safely shut. The gelding raced away from her. Usually, Amy would have taken him to the middle of the arena and chased him away with the lunge line but Loup hadn't given her the chance. He was making his rejection of her plain and clear.

When the gelding reached the far end of the corral he lifted his head and let out a loud whinny, clearly seeking company of the four-legged kind. *Because he doesn't trust the two-legged variety.*

"Here goes," Amy said to Will as he climbed up onto the gate. "Wish me luck."

She turned and walked up to Loup, who was staring over the fence. When he swung his head around to look at her, she flicked the lead line. "Go!"

With a surprised snort, Loup wheeled away from her. Amy hurried into the middle of the corral so she could keep him running.

As she watched him circle the arena again and again, Amy realized she was watching a horse who didn't just love to run, but one who was born to run. Loup's stride beat effortlessly over the dusty surface and Amy knew she'd have to drive him faster to tire him. She flicked the line just behind his heels, and Loup put on an extra burst of speed. As she watched Loup gallop around and around she had to face how deep his mistrust of humans was. *He's not going to let go. He'll keep going until he drops.* If the option was between putting his trust in her or dropping from exhaustion, he'd pick exhaustion.

Amy thought of Loup's single-minded nature and just how focused he could be. The personality that made him such a fantastic ranch horse was now working against him. He stumbled twice as tiredness began to set in. But he still didn't stop. "Please, Loup, give it up," Amy murmured. She wished she could make him see she wasn't a threat. She wished she could make him understand that if he didn't start trusting again he was going to be put down. She dug her fingernails into her palms as sweat began to streak Loup's neck and flanks.

She had known it was too early to work with him. He had needed more time before he was ready to take this step. She faltered and lowered the hand that was driving the gelding forward. At once Loup began to slow his pace.

Believe in yourself and so will he. Amy could hear her mom's voice as if she were still alive and standing beside her, encouraging her never to quit no matter what.

"I'm not going to give up on you." Amy gritted her teeth and flicked the line again. And then she recognized the sign she'd almost given up hope of seeing. He lowered his head and began working his jaws in a chewing action. Amy felt relief wash over her. Loup was finally beginning to lower his barriers. She kept him running but as Loup began to ask to go slower, she allowed him to slacken his pace. His inside ear was riveted on her, and Amy knew now was the moment she had to trust Loup just as she was asking him to trust her.

She dropped the lunge line down and stepped ahead

of his movement. Loup immediately took the chance she was offering to slow to a trot and then a walk. Finally, he stopped and looked at her. Amy held her breath. *Please walk toward me, Loup, please.*

Loup paused for several heartbeats and then swung away from the fence to head toward Amy.

She wanted to shout with happiness. "Keep coming, there's a good boy," she said, slowly turning her back. Now all she needed was for Loup to come up to her and follow her wherever she walked. She would know then that he had broken through his barrier of fear and pain and truly put his trust in her.

Out of the corner of her eye, Amy saw a brown blur as a wild rabbit streaked across the arena. There was a snarl and a bark as one of the ranch dogs squeezed under the fence in hot pursuit. Loup let out a frightened whinny.

Amy spun around to see the gelding racing toward the gate. In his terror, Loup was heading blindly for his only route of escape. There was no way he was going to be trapped in the corral with a snarling animal. But Amy could see from his approach that he couldn't possibly clear the gate.

"Will!" she cried. "Stop him!"

Chapter Eleven

Will's reaction was lightning fast. He didn't risk stepping in front of Loup and getting crushed between horse and gate but opened the gate just wide enough to tempt Loup to go through instead of jumping. At the same time, he made the opening as narrow as possible to force Loup to slow down. As the palomino twisted through the gap, Will grabbed his halter.

"Nice job." Amy was breathless when she reached them.

Loup's flanks were heaving and the whites of his eyes were wide with fright.

"It's going well then?" called a sarcastic voice.

Amy groaned inwardly. She hadn't noticed Mike arrive.

The wrangler walked over and stopped a short distance away while he glared at Loup.

Loup reared up in the air as the German shepherd ran up to Mike, his plumy tail wagging.

"Whoa!" Amy cried, trying to calm Loup. "Can you take the dog away, please?"

"So it's not just people that horse doesn't like anymore, it's dogs, too! And you think he's got something to offer this ranch?" Mike stooped to make a fuss over the dog. "I think I'll go have a word with Hank and Stan about this. He could have seriously hurt someone or one of the livestock just now." With that parting shot, he sauntered off, with the German shepherd running at his heels.

Amy stared after him, trying to ignore the possibility that Mike had deliberately walked by with the dog when they were working with Loup. It would have been easy to guess that a large dog might unsettle him after the attack by a mountain lion.

Will let out a rather shaky whistle. "What do you want to do with Loup now?" He rubbed the palomino's nose as Loup gave a heavy sigh.

"I think he should go back to his stall, and we'll spend some time doing T-touch again," Amy told him, biting back her frustration. She'd been so close to joining up with the troubled horse but now he was as far away as ever.

"I'm sorry." Will reached out and squeezed her arm. His face was pale, and Amy realized it wasn't just from the scare. *Loup means a lot to him.*

"Mike won't really go to Hank and Stan, will he?" she asked.

"Oh, he will, but Stan won't listen to him. He knows what a great horse Loup was and is really hoping you're going to get through to him. I guess that Hank won't be happy about what just happened, but he respects Stan enough to keep to the agreed date. . . ."

"He was about to join up with me when the dog ran into the corral," Amy reminded him. "We'll bring him down again tomorrow, early in the morning before breakfast, and try it again." She'd never seen Will so subdued. It was her turn to squeeze his arm. "We've still got time left. I'll get through to Loup, I promise."

But as they walked the palomino back to his stall, Amy wrestled with her own doubts. Loup now had bad associations with join-up. It had been hard enough getting him to respond to her today. Maybe tomorrow he really would choose to collapse rather than put his trust in her.

Loup snorted, and Amy reached up to drape her arm over his neck. She was pleased when he didn't object to her closeness as they walked quietly back to his stall.

"I'm starting to see what a dumb thing it was to say he'd be ready for the cattle drive on Saturday," Will said.

"Not dumb, maybe just overly optimistic," Amy said gently. But silently she agreed that the idea of Loup on the cattle drive in two days' time couldn't be more out of the question.

After they had washed Loup down, put extra straw in his bed, and massaged him with lavender oil, they headed back to the bunkhouses. Amy was longing for a shower. She was feeling hot and sticky and ached all over.

As they walked by the corrals they saw some of the ranch hands climbing into two open-backed Jeeps. Corey stood up and waved. "Hey, guys, we're going Tucson dipping, you coming?"

"Come on!" Will grabbed Amy's hand as the drivers of the Jeeps started the engines.

Amy hesitated. "Tucson dipping?"

"Trust me." Will smiled. "You'll be glad you came." He took her hand and pulled her over to the nearest Jeep. They clambered into the back and squeezed in between four wranglers Amy had seen at mealtimes but hadn't met, along with Scooby and Max.

"How did the riding lesson go?" she asked.

"I had my horse cornering like it was on rails," Scooby replied. "Hal wants me to come back and enter the Tucson rodeo, but I told him that school's got to come first."

Hal knocked his Stetson away from his face so Amy could see the amused expression in his pale blue eyes. "What Scooby means is, he crashed and burned the first, second, fourth, and last barrels, and we want to enter him in the rodeo as the comic relief."

There was a roar of laughter from the other wranglers as Hal leaned forward and slapped Scooby on the back.

"I have photographic evidence," Max agreed. "Still, you have one last day of practice before the decision's made about you coming on the cattle drive, huh, Scoob?"

"The only reason we crashed those barrels was because I made a slight miscalculation with my precision measurements. You wait and see what we do tomorrow," Scooby retorted.

"What about you guys? How did it go with Loup?" Max asked, grabbing onto the side of the Jeep as they bumped over the rocky terrain.

Amy and Will exchanged glances. "I'd say we're about as far along as Scooby," Amy replied. "At least we still have one more day of practice."

"I heard Loup spooked real bad at one of the dogs." One of the female ranch hands sitting opposite Amy leaned forward. "I'm Fallon, by the way."

Amy smiled ruefully as they shook hands. "It didn't take Mike long to spread the news."

"Well, everyone knows how much he hates Loup after Sam's accident. But he's got good reason." Fallon narrowed her green eyes. "Mike says what you're doing is a total waste of time."

Something about her abrupt manner made Amy feel uncomfortable. "It sounds as if you do, too."

Fallon shrugged. "You must be good at what you do or you wouldn't be here. I wouldn't expect you to question the way I rope, herd, drive, or cull the steers so I'm not going to question what you do. But I can't help thinking you're working with a pretty tight schedule."

"I'd have to agree," Amy said, and thought she caught a glimmer of a smile from Fallon.

"Maybe it would have been better for Loup to live his last few days in peace rather than being totally stressed out?" Fallon raised her eyebrows.

Amy thought indignantly of the hours she and Will had spent massaging Loup and doing everything they could to relax him. Fallon was talking about just one tense incident in all that time. "I don't think we are stressing him," she said tightly.

Fallon shook her head. "Don't worry, Amy. I'm only expressing an opinion."

Amy held her gaze. "Ditto."

"Time out, girls. We're here," Will interrupted. He jumped up and grabbed the Jeep's overhead bar to help him balance.

They didn't seem to be anywhere in particular. The desert stretched into the distance with the heat dancing over it in a shimmering haze. Will pulled Amy to her feet and as they waited their turn to get off the truck, he whispered into her ear. "Fallon's cool once you get to know her. She's just really direct and it takes some getting used to."

Amy nodded and watched Fallon leap off the truck onto Hal's back. She held one hand in the air and whooped as he spun around, pretending to try to dislodge her like an angry steer. Fallon then jumped off Hal's back and began to climb the steps of a huge elevated circular steel tank that was used to store water.

Amy realized they'd come out here to swim. And they were going to swim in a water tower.

Fallon balanced on the edge of the tank before diving fully clothed into the water.

We're swimming in our clothes? Amy watched as everyone joined Fallon amid shouts of laughter and splashing.

"Are you coming or watching?" Will nudged her.

"Coming," Amy nodded. She kicked off her boots and socks and climbed up the ladder beside Will.

At the top he turned and took her hand. "One, two, three, go!"

They leaped into the water, and Amy gasped as the warm surface gave way to much colder depths. It took her a few seconds to adjust as she splashed vigorously, kicking out to cover Will in a spray of water.

Will responded by diving under the surface and grabbing at her legs. He dunked her once before swimming quickly away.

"Amy!" Leila and Kirsten waved to her from the opposite side of the water tank, but as Amy went to swim across, her way was blocked by Mike. Although the wrangler had his back to her it was obvious he'd blocked her on purpose as he began to talk in a loud voice to a couple of the other ranch hands who were treading water close by.

"Hey guys, I have a question for you. What's the best thing to do with a horse that's lost it? A) shoot it? B) send it to the bucking bronco category at the Tucson Rodeo? or C)" — he paused for dramatic effect — "shoot it?"

Amy's cheeks burned with anger but before she could react, there was a splash and Mike suddenly disappeared underneath the water. Fallon surfaced beside Amy and winked at her. When Mike reappeared, furiously spitting out water, Fallon called out, "I have another option. D) drown it, but only if it's dumb enough to let you get ahold of its legs!"

Amy burst out laughing.

"You can't let the guys around here get away with anything or they'll start thinking they rule the roost," Fallon said dismissively.

Mike glared at Amy before he swam away from her to climb out of the water tank.

Amy sighed. It wasn't going to be easy working with Loup when Mike seemed determined to undermine her efforts. All she could hope was that by taking Loup down to the corral early enough in the morning, Mike wouldn't be aware of their second attempt at join-up.

❧

Loup's hay net hadn't been touched all night and his coat was matted with dried sweat. Amy frowned. Yesterday's incident in the corral had clearly had a deep effect on him.

Will hadn't arrived yet, so she decided to spend some time grooming Loup. By the time Will joined her, the horse's coat was spotless and Amy was gently massaging lavender oil into his neck. She had to believe that the remedies she was putting into his water were helping along with the regular massages. But it would have been so much better if she could have delayed joining up until she sensed he was ready.

Loup gave out a gentle nicker as Will bent his head to blow into his nostrils.

Amy smiled. It was the first indication Loup had given of welcoming a person's company. "I think maybe you should lead him down to the corral," she said, handing Will Loup's lead rein.

"Are you sure?" When Amy nodded, Will clicked his tongue and led Loup out of the stall. After a moment's hesitation, the palomino followed him.

Amy was reminded again of Will's natural gift with

animals. He was handling Loup like he'd been around horses for his whole life, as comfortably as Ty would have been.

When they reached the corral, Loup walked with Will to the center but as soon as the halter was off the gelding cantered away. "Do you want to stay with me while I try to join up with him?" Amy asked. The join-up was important for Loup's sake, but it would be wonderful if Will could finally see what she'd described in action.

"I'd love to," Will told her.

Amy took a deep breath and flicked the lunge line at Loup. The gelding responded by galloping away from the line. "You might think that he's ignoring me and just concentrating on running away from the lead line, but if I do this," she stepped in front of Loup's movement and he slowed his pace, "and then I do this," she stepped back and Loup put on a fresh spurt of speed, "you can see how closely his movements are influenced by mine."

Will whistled softly. "That's amazing."

Amy nodded. "See his inside ear and eye? They're totally focused on me. He can't figure out why I'm chasing him but at the moment he's happy to run. He and I don't belong together and he's quick to fear me. But when he starts to get tired, he'll start to think that he'd rather be with me than running away from me."

She fell silent for a while, watching Loup's steady

stride as he circled the compound. Would he run and run, determined not to put his faith in her and have that faith shattered?

But even as she questioned the gelding's nature he dropped his head lower. Amy stared in astonishment. She knew without doubt the signs of a horse asking to stop running, but she still questioned it for a second. She would have sworn that Loup was going to fight her all the way today. But as the gelding began to open and close his mouth, Amy knew that he was prepared to put his trust in her for a second time. "He's showing us that he wants to join us, to be with us instead of being an outsider," she murmured. Gently she dropped her aggressive stance and turned her back on Loup. Will copied her.

She heard Loup's canter become a trot and then the four beats of trotting thudded to a halt. Her throat tightened as she heard the most wonderful sound: the soft pad of Loup's hooves as the gelding walked across the sand toward her. Amy's heart thumped as he drew nearer and she felt his nose rest on her shoulder.

Amy took three steps forward, and Loup followed her as closely as her own shadow. Wherever she went he stayed with her until she rewarded him by turning around and slipping her arms around his neck.

"Awesome," said Will, coming to join them. "Totally awesome."

Amy nodded, too happy to speak. There was real hope for Loup now. He'd taken the biggest step by choosing to trust and from here on she could build on its solid foundation.

The rising sun split the sky with orange-and-gold light. It was the dawn of a new day and, hopefully, the dawn of a new beginning for Loup.

Chapter Twelve

Amy's feelings of elation were soon replaced with more practical concerns. As she and Will waited for Stan to arrive for their morning's veterinary work, she began to plan a schedule for Loup. She had to get a rider on his back by the end of the day; Hank wouldn't be impressed by Loup just following her around the corral. He had told Will that unless the horse was able to be ridden, he was to be put down Saturday morning before the cattle drive.

Amy's thoughts were broken by Stan pulling up. "Ah, my workers are all ready and waiting, that's what I like to see."

Amy liked the veterinarian tremendously. He had a quiet, calm manner that animals responded to, and she admired the way he always treated each one with respect.

He didn't come across as thinking that animals were just his "job."

"We're ranch-based again today. We've got to worm the cattle." Stan spoke apologetically, but Amy was more than happy to stay on the ranch. She was learning more than she'd ever dreamed possible in just a couple of days. "You're welcome to come out on my rounds with me this afternoon, but I know you've got ranch chores and your work with Loup," Stan went on as he led the way down to the corrals. "How's that going?"

"Really well," Will said enthusiastically. "I got to watch my first join-up today and it was unreal! It's really made me appreciate the importance of learning about animal psychology as well as physiology."

"We've still got quite a few hurdles to overcome before tomorrow," Amy added. "But Loup's taken an important step toward showing that he's prepared to trust people again."

Fallon and a crowd of wranglers were waiting in the corral to assist the vet. To worm the cows, each one had to be cut out from the other cattle and driven into one of the crushes that opened on to a second empty corral. The ranch hands were going to work in teams of four. Two would herd the cow into the crush, one would administer the wormer while the other member of the team helped hold the cow and then released it into the corral.

Amy was glad of the protection offered by the Stetson Ty had given her. It was hot and the sun was strong. She and Will were working with Stan and Fallon.

"Here, Amy, you can do this first." Stan handed her what looked like a rifle. Amy's mouth went dry as she took hold of the plastic bolus gun, which felt as light as a toy in her hands. She hadn't expected to be first up. Stan showed her how to load the bolus into the gun. The rounded plastic pellet felt surprisingly heavy. "Someone will hold the cow's head up so its throat is nice and straight and all you have to do is load the bolus, slide the butt a little down the cow's throat and pull the trigger. The pellet will shoot straight into its stomach, and the cow won't feel a thing. OK?"

"Race you," Fallon called across to the other teams. She was perched on the top rail of the crush and the moment the first cow scrambled in, she had its head up in one smooth movement.

Amy fumbled with the bolus and cursed as it fell onto the floor. Will had it washed off in the trough and back in her hand in a matter of moments. Amy steeled herself for a sharp remark from Fallon but when she met the other girl's eyes, Fallon winked. "Just lulling the boys into a false sense of security, right?"

"Right," Amy said with a grin, feeling a new sense of determination.

Fallon lifted the cow's head up again, and Amy slid

the gun in and fired. The pellet slipped into the cow's stomach, and the animal did nothing more than widen its eyes slightly in surprise.

"Watch out boys, we're taking the lead," Fallon called as the first cow was released and the next was driven into the pen.

Her enthusiasm was infectious and Amy felt the appeal of ranch life more than ever. She'd never trade Heartland for a cattle ranch, but she could see why many of the hired hands who came to Shallow Creek Ranch never left. *It's way more than a job. It's a life that grabs hold of you and doesn't let go.*

❧

Amy didn't think she'd ever worked so hard. Right after lunch they were back in the corrals to help with hoof trimming. The cows were caught and penned while the ranch hands got to work cutting back and rasping their hooves.

"Here." Mike handed Amy a rope. "Tie this around his front leg so he can't kick me with the back."

Amy took the rope and struggled to tie it around the steer's leg.

"What are you doing?" A shadow fell over her and, glancing over her shoulder, Amy saw Hank staring down with a frown.

"Tying the steer so it can't kick out . . ." She trailed off as she caught sight of Mike's grin. He'd deliberately set her up just as Hank was coming along.

Amy set her lips in a tight line as Hank took the rope from her and coiled it. She felt like an idiot.

Mike spoke up. "It's not her fault, Hank."

Amy stopped and stared. She couldn't believe Mike was going to do the decent thing and own up.

"It's probably another 'alternative method.'" Mike smirked at her in an open challenge. "Best stick with the real world, girl."

Amy lifted her chin. "Well, the alternative methods haven't done badly so far. In fact, I was going to invite you both down to the corral after supper tonight to see Loup's progress." She turned to Hank. "You said I should let you know when I was ready to get on Loup."

Hank played with the match he was chewing. "OK," he agreed. "We'll come by around eight."

Amy didn't have to look at Mike to sense he was seething, but right now she had more important things to worry about. Tonight was her only chance. If Loup wouldn't allow himself to be ridden, then when tomorrow morning came, Stan would have no alternative but to put him down.

"What I don't understand is why you asked Mike to come." Will looked concerned as they walked down to

Loup's stall. They had a few free hours between finishing the hoof trimming and supper, and Amy had decided to join up with Loup again. She needed to build on the initial bond between them before she tried to ride him later on.

"Oh, you know, keep your friends close and your enemies closer," Amy said. "At least with Mike there, it stops him from accidentally wandering by with one of the ranch dogs."

Will's expression cleared. "Right, now I understand."

They walked to the quad where there were horses looking out over almost every door. They were having a rest day before the cattle drive tomorrow. Amy stopped to pat Demon, Hank's horse. Contrary to his name, he had a gentle, calm nature and snuffled hopefully at her hands. "Here," she said, offering him one of the horse cookies that she'd brought.

As Demon crunched on the cookie, Loup's head appeared over the adjoining door. Seeing Amy and Will, he pulled back his upper lip and then let out a whinny in welcome.

Amy and Will grinned at each other.

"Even more good news, he's emptied his hay net," Will announced when they walked into Loup's stall.

Amy held out a horse cookie for Loup. "Want to try one?" Loup stretched out his neck and sniffed the treat before lipping it off her palm.

Amy reached up to tease a strand of hay from Loup's forelock and was pleased when he didn't flinch away. She slipped his halter on, noting how much more accepting he was compared to the previous day.

"Walk on, boy." She clicked her tongue, and Loup calmly followed her out to the yard.

Demon whickered to Loup as he walked past and both geldings touched noses to say hello.

"He might be anti-human and anti-dog but at least he's not anti-horse," Will joked, "because that really would have been a problem!"

Once they were in the corral, Loup walked calmly to the center and this time, when Amy unclipped his halter, the gelding didn't canter away. "Go on!" Amy laughed. "You know what to do." She flicked the lunge line at Loup's quarters and he cantered obediently to the outside of the corral.

He galloped around and around, his tail streaming like a banner. When he lowered his head and began opening and closing his mouth, Will gave Amy a thumbs-up from the gate.

She waited for Loup to make a chewing action with his jaws before she stopped chasing him. The moment she dropped her arm, the horse slowed his canter and stopped. He turned his head to look at Amy and she was struck by how noble he looked. He needed to heal and return to his former life — the life he belonged to. Amy suddenly longed to see him on the cattle drive the next day, doing the job he was born to do.

She slowly turned her back and waited for the sweet sound of Loup's footfalls on the sand. When he bumped his nose into her back, an idea formed in Amy's head. She didn't want Loup's first riding session to be in front of Hank and Mike in which he might pick up on the feeling of pressure. She wanted it to be now. She turned to praise the palomino and looked at his broad inviting back. She knew she'd promised that she'd go to Hank when she was ready to ride him, but she'd done that, hadn't she?

Amy hesitated. Slipping onto him now would probably freak him out a lot less than putting all of his tack on and mounting him in front of an audience. Bareback riding was the most natural form of being ridden for any horse.

She clipped on Loup's lead rope and knotted it around his neck. Putting her hand on his neck and withers, she sprang onto his back. Loup stiffened and then shied. Amy let her legs hang low and used gravity and balance to keep her on.

Loup shot forward into a stiff-backed trot, and Amy tried to move naturally with him. "Steady, boy," she soothed. Loup's trot became a canter and then, without warning, he twisted into the air. Amy knew it would be foolish to stay on for any longer. She quickly slid off his back, keeping a hand on his rope to steady him.

As soon as she was off, Loup began to calm down, but he was clearly still stressed. Amy looked at him in pity as he broke into a sweat and began to tremble.

"I'm so sorry, boy," she murmured. "I know that I'm rushing you, but my back's against the wall."

"Are you OK?" Will was jogging toward them. "I thought he was going to buck you off."

"I'm not surprised," Amy said ruefully. "I knew I was pushing it, so I can't blame him." She patted Loup's neck. "After what he went through he just can't cope with the idea of being ridden again."

Will stared at her in dismay. "But that means Hank will have him destroyed tomorrow."

"We've got one more stab at it later," Amy reminded him. But inside she was beginning to lose all confidence that the palomino would come through for them — and for himself — that evening.

Amy slipped away from the bunkhouse before supper, needing a little time alone. She found herself walking toward the barn where Hank kept his horses. The ranch owner had told her to visit them anytime.

When she walked into the barn, the horses were all in for the night. A radio was playing and Nicky was pushing a wheelbarrow down the aisle.

"Amy, right?" Nicky said. "Hank said you'd be back."

"Hi." Amy smiled. "Is it OK if I say hi to the horses?"

"No problem," Nicky told her. "Help yourself."

All of the horses had just been fed, and Amy paused for a moment to enjoy the familiar sound of munching. In one of the middle stalls was the yearling she had seen running around in the field. He was still sharing a box with his mother, and Amy smiled as he finished his own feed and reached out to sniff the mare's bucket. His mother gave him a gentle nip to chastise him and the yearling reluctantly backed off.

"Here, boy," Amy called, holding out a cookie.

The yearling moved over the straw to sniff at her hand. He thrust his small muzzle into her palm and snatched up the treat. Amy reached out to scratch his nose but the yearling was too quick for her and whisked away and back to his mother.

Amy watched them for a while longer and then went to look at the other horses. One of the most striking horses was a few stalls down. She was about sixteen hands with a beautiful, intelligent head. The mare's shoulders and hips were long and sloping and Amy could see that she was the result of careful quality breeding.

As the mare snuffled Amy's hand, she felt a surge of homesickness. She wondered what Ty was doing right now. Was he out with his friends? The Heartland horses would be settled in for the night. She pictured Spindle and Sundance quietly grazing alongside each other.

Maybe if she called the farm she'd be in time to catch Ty before he left.

She pulled out her cell phone and dialed home. After three rings, Grandpa answered. "Hey, honey. How are you?"

"Good, thanks," Amy told him. "Except for missing you all."

"We're missing you, too," Jack told her. "Ty left about five minutes ago. You'll have to call his cell if you want to talk to him."

"OK." Amy hesitated. "Grandpa?"

"Yes, sweetheart?"

"I'm going to ride Loup tonight for Hank, the ranch owner."

"That's great," Jack replied. "He's doing well, then?"

"That's the problem. I don't think he is. I've never been this unsure about a horse before. But tonight's my last chance. If it doesn't work out . . ." Her voice broke.

"Hey, is this my granddaughter I'm talking to?" Jack said gently. "Listen, sweetheart, you're miles away from home in a new place and you're probably exhausted. Just don't forget that you're Marion's daughter and you have her gift. Part of that gift is believing against all the odds. It makes you special. It makes you who you are. My Amy."

Amy's eyes filled with tears at the love in her grandfather's voice. She wished she shared his unshakable confidence in herself.

"Don't doubt yourself, sweetheart," he went on. "If you do, then Loup will sense it and doubt you, too. The reason why your mom healed so many horses was that she didn't ever think she couldn't. Now you go and do your thing, and I want you to call me back later and say just four words, okay?"

"What four words?" Amy whispered.

"'We did it, Grandpa,'" Jack replied. "I love you, Amy."

"I love you, too, Grandpa. Very much." Hanging up, Amy pushed the back of her hands against her eyes. She took a deep breath. Grandpa was right. She was Marion Fleming's daughter and she was going to use everything her mom had taught her to break through to Loup.

"Steady, boy," Amy whispered as she unclipped Loup's halter. The gelding was fully tacked in his western saddle and bridle and his tension was palpable. "You and I are going to do this tonight. Against all the odds."

She closed her eyes for a moment and remembered the time almost five years ago when her mom, her face full of pride, had stood alongside her and shown her how to join up. *I need you now, Mom. I wish you were here beside me, talking me through things the way you did with Sundance.*

Thinking of her mom filled her with renewed strength and in a clear voice she said to Loup, "Go!"

Will was sitting on the gate, and Hank and Mike were standing beside him. Hank's face was unreadable as he watched the gelding run, his reins secured by his throat lash to prevent them from trailing.

Despite Loup's anxiety at being tacked up, he went through the motions of join-up like an old hand. When Amy allowed him into the center of the arena with her, she spent much longer having him follow her. Even if riding him went wrong, at least Hank would be able to see that Loup was beginning to place his confidence in people again by the way he shadowed her every movement around the corral.

When she stopped near the gate, Hank nodded. "That's impressive work."

Amy's heart soared. Maybe Hank wouldn't want Loup pushed to the next stage after all. But with his next words, her hopes plummeted. "But I won't make up my mind until I see what he's like with a rider on his back."

Amy glanced at Will and saw his eyes darken with worry. Loup took his confidence from being handled on the ground, not from a rider. Amy needed to shift that confidence but she couldn't see how to do it without freaking out Loup.

An idea quickly formed in her mind. "Will, can you come with me, please?"

Will frowned but didn't question her until they were out of Hank and Mike's earshot.

"Do you remember everything I did when I joined up with Loup, and you were with me?" Amy asked, halting the gelding in the middle of the ring. She unbuckled his throat lash to release the reins.

"Sure. What are you planning?"

"I want you to join up with Loup while I'm on his back," Amy told him. Seeing his look of doubt, she rushed on. "Loup's confident and comfortable with join-up. I'm hoping he'll almost forget I'm on his back because I'm not going to try to ride him. I'm just going to be a passenger on board to begin with. His focus will be on you, not on me. Please, Will. I think it's his only chance."

Will's blue eyes filled with determination. "Then we've got to go for it."

Amy grinned. "Can you give me a leg up so I can get on him as quietly as possible?"

Will boosted her into the saddle and then immediately flicked the lunge line at Loup's quarters so the horse couldn't concentrate on the fact that he had a rider on his back.

Loup galloped faster around the arena than when he had during the first join-up, and Amy hoped that Hank wouldn't notice and deduce that the palomino wasn't happy about the fact that he had a rider on his back. She interfered with Loup as little as possible. Although she held the reins, she didn't use them. She needed Loup to forget about her and concentrate on Will. Part of her longed to mutter soothing words to the gelding but that would only take his attention off Will, so she held back and prayed that Loup would soon settle.

After two circuits she felt a change in the palomino. His inside ear flickered toward Will who was calling at him to keep moving. *He's focusing on Will, not me*, Amy thought with relief.

Loup's pace slowed as Will stepped ahead of his movement and as they cantered past the gate, Amy noticed that Fallon had joined Mike and Hank.

Now, Will! Amy thought when the gelding lowered his neck and began to chew his mouth. She could really feel the difference in Loup. All of the tension had gone out of his body. She could sense that his entire focus was on Will in the center of the ring.

Will dropped the rope and, when Loup halted, he slowly turned his back to them.

Amy felt a rush of excitement as Loup, totally unguided by her, swung away from the outside fence and walked calmly over the sand to Will. The gelding stretched out his neck and nudged Will, who turned around and walked three paces forward. Loup matched every step and when Will walked in a full circle, Loup unhesitatingly followed. Finally, Will turned to face them. His eyes were bright with emotion as he rubbed Loup between the eyes. "That was the most amazing thing ever," he murmured. He looked up at Amy. "Thank you."

Amy nodded, her throat aching. She knew exactly what Will was feeling right now. "There's just one more bridge for us to cross," she said, shortening her reins. "Wish me luck."

"I don't think I need to," Will said softly. "You have a talent that has nothing to do with luck."

Amy squeezed gently to get Loup to step away from Will. The horse ignored her. Leaning forward, she stroked his neck and talked in his ear. "Hey, gorgeous boy. You and I have something to prove now. We're going to do it together. I'm going to be with you every step of the way and I'm not going to leave you or let you down, I swear."

She put more pressure on the girth and clicked with her tongue. "Walk on, Loup."

Reluctantly, the palomino stepped away from Will and walked over to the fence where Amy asked him to trot. As she sat deep into his long-legged stride, Amy felt him tense underneath the saddle. She kept her legs close against him, willing him to believe that she wasn't going to desert him, that she was with him every stride of the way. His spine started to relax and finally Amy felt him moving with her rather than against her.

The last major barrier had been broken and when she asked him for a canter, he carried her around the arena without any fuss. After a couple of circuits, Amy guided him over to the gate where Hank, Mike, and Fallon were waiting. Will had joined them, too.

"Very touching." Mike spoke first. "But no trick riding is going to convince me that horse is reliable. It's all very well riding him in an enclosed corral, but how's he going to react out doing the real work? He'll turn tail and bolt the moment the first small four-legged animal comes into sight."

"Why don't you just lay off, Mike?" Fallon asked. "Amy and Will have worked a small miracle here and you know it."

Hank hadn't taken his eyes off Loup the whole time they were talking, but he suddenly turned his piercing glance on Amy. "They're both right in a way. You have worked wonders with the horse, but is it something that can last outside a corral?" He drummed his fingers on the gate. "I tell you what I'm going to do. I'm going to tell Stan not to come by in the morning."

Amy felt a rush of elation. But she sensed there was more coming.

"I'm going to take Loup out on the cattle drive with us tomorrow. He's an old hand and shouldn't have a problem if what you've just shown us is genuine. The drive will be the test of whether Loup is really fit to live."

At Hank's words, Mike spat onto the ground and stalked away.

Fallon rolled her eyes into the air before hurrying after him.

"Is it OK if I'm the one to ride him?" Amy asked.

Hank nodded. "Sure. Trust me, nobody wants Loup to come through tomorrow more than I do." He stuck out his hand. "Well done, Amy. You've proved a lot of us wrong just by being able to get on that horse."

Amy returned the handshake. "Thanks." *But it's not over yet,* she thought, watching the ranch owner walk away.

"We did it!" Will told her, his face lit up. "Don't think about tomorrow, just concentrate on what the three of us accomplished tonight." He held out his arms and Amy pulled off her stirrups and jumped into them to give him a victory hug.

When he let her go so she could hug Loup, Amy handed Will his reins. "Do you want to take him back to his stall? I'll be with you in a minute but there's something important I have to do first."

She held open the gate for Will and Loup to walk through and then fished her cell phone out of her pocket.

The phone at Heartland was answered almost immediately. "Hello?"

Amy took a breath and then spoke the four best words in the world: "We did it, Grandpa."

Chapter Thirteen

Amy and Will sponged Loup down and gave him an extra-special feed with chopped carrots and apples as a reward. Amy added some Rock Rose to deal with the terror that might come back to Loup when they took him out into the environment where his attack took place.

When she finally got to call Ty, it was dark. She stood on the veranda of the bunkhouse and waited for him to answer.

"Hello?" His voice sounded sleepy.

"I'm so sorry, did I wake you?" Amy had forgotten all about the time difference.

"It's fine." Ty's voice lost its grogginess. "How did it go with Loup tonight?"

"It couldn't have been better." Amy described the whole thing to him.

"Thinking of using join-up while you were riding him was a great idea, Amy. It was exactly the right call," Ty told her. "Good luck tomorrow. I have a feeling he's going to be fine."

"Thanks, Ty." Amy said good night but when she hung up she felt a distance separating her from Ty that was more than the miles between them. She sighed and figured she was just worried about riding Loup in the cattle drive. She decided to turn in for the night even though it was on the early side. She wished she could share Ty's confidence that Loup would be fine the next day.

As she lay in bed a short time later, she tried to visualize what she wanted to happen the next day. The last thought she had before she fell asleep was of Loup, in full western tack, galloping behind the cattle. His tail was streaming out like a banner as he covered mile after mile in complete harmony with his surroundings.

Early the next morning the ranch was buzzing. Amy had eaten one of her grandpa's muffins for breakfast, unable to face a cooked meal. After a few days the muffins were starting to get a little stale, but they were so good she didn't even mind. She pressed her hand over her stomach, feeling her nerves kick in just as if she were about to ride in a competition.

Scooby was carrying tack into the stall two doors down from Loup. He gave her a cheery smile and she grinned, pleased that he'd passed his riding levels and was allowed out on the drive. She got Loup's tack from the tack room. Half the racks were already empty, and it was quite a squeeze trying to get to her saddle and bridle through the crowd of ranch hands who were all trying to do the same thing.

Amy tried hard not to let her nervousness show as she groomed Loup and tacked him up. She double-checked that he was comfortable with his saddle, pulling out his forelegs to make sure there was no skin trapped under the girth. She didn't want anything to set him off.

Before she led Loup out she spent a moment with her head pressed against his. "I know today is going to ask a lot of you, but you are one of the most courageous horses I've ever known and I totally believe that you can do this."

Loup nuzzled her shoulder, and Amy pulled back to tease his forelock out from under his headband. The yard was echoing with the sound of shod hooves. "Here we go," Amy said, leading Loup out to join the other horses.

The gelding stood still for Amy to mount him but skittered away when she landed on his back. Amy was slightly unseated and had to hold on to his mane for balance. "Easy, Loup."

Mike rode by on his buckskin. "Maybe you should stay home. You're going to be facing much bigger trials than mounting a pony."

Amy bit back her response. She needed to be totally focused on Loup right now, not on some silly fight with Mike.

"Here, Amy, stick close by me until he settles." Will rode up alongside her on Domino, the black-and-white paint horse he'd been given to ride. He leaned forward to pat Loup's shoulder. "Hey, fella. You're surrounded by friends."

Amy settled into the deep Western saddle, glad of how much more comfortable it was than riding English style. "Let's go," she said, squeezing Loup forward.

Loup fell in with the other ranch hands and horses making their way down to the corrals where more than a thousand head of cattle were waiting. Amy couldn't believe how much noise the herd was making.

Almost all the ranch hands were mounted. A few were standing at the gates waiting to release the cattle and those who were bringing the provisions for the night were packed into Jeeps. Amy had camped in a tent but had never slept out under the stars before, yet right now she couldn't bring herself to be excited at the prospect, even with her grandpa's bedroll to keep her comfortable. All she could think about was how Loup was going to react to a whole day under a saddle.

The cattle dogs were up front with Hank and the senior wranglers. Amy was happy to hold Loup at the back, away from the main action. The horse was fighting her hands, his back rigid, and Amy felt that any more stress would send him into a fit.

Suddenly, the gates were opened and the cattle charged out, kicking up a huge cloud of orange dust. Dog barks mingled with wranglers' shouts and the cattle bellowing. Amy felt Loup bunch underneath her. "Easy, boy," she soothed, glad of Will close against them.

"Are you OK?" he shouted.

"I'll be glad when we finally get going. I think once he's moving he'll have more to occupy his mind," Amy called back.

It seemed like forever before they were able to move and when they did, Loup began prancing nervously.

When they rode out onto the pastureland, Amy sensed that all Loup wanted was to turn and run. She held him firmly. "Steady, boy. I'm not leaving you, we're doing this together."

By the time they'd left the pasture behind and were riding over desert, Amy was tired from fighting Loup. The gelding was totally wound up, and Amy felt he was on the verge of turning his anxiety on to her. His tail was clamped down tightly, showing that he wasn't relaxed. All Amy could do was to ride him as strongly but sympathetically as possible. Join-up was all about showing the horse that the person was stronger and the one in control. She had to remind Loup of that now with firm riding.

Will brought Domino up alongside Loup and, to her surprise, Max appeared on Tahoe, the cow pony he'd been given to ride.

Feeling the security of the two horses close to him, Loup calmed a little. Amy smiled her thanks at Max and then glanced at Will. He had formed a bond with Loup every bit as close as the one she had, and Amy knew that his voice and presence were soothing the gelding.

Amy leaned forward and murmured into Loup's ear. "Start trusting me, Loup, please."

Loup's ear flickered back, and Amy increased the pressure on her reins a little to underline her promise that she was there, in control, keeping him safe.

The pace ahead picked up and for the first time, Amy felt her horse settle into an easier stride. Max rode increasingly wide of her and, after a while, so did Will. Amy began to relax and take her mind a little off Loup and focus on the job at hand, though she continued to ride the gelding confidently so he wouldn't doubt that she was with him the whole way.

The cattle were kicking up a sandstorm up front, and Amy was glad that she wasn't in the thick of it along with the other wranglers. She now understood why they were wearing bandannas around their necks that could be pulled up over their mouths.

Just before noon, they left the sandy terrain behind and rode into a valley. The gentle slopes were covered in the sort of trees Amy would expect to find in an orchard, and they fought for space with other lush vegetation.

As they rode through a narrow canyon, a shower of small stones from high above spooked Loup. With a frightened snort, he careened ahead, cutting through some of the other ponies. Amy was terrified that he was going to charge past the senior wranglers and run into the tight band of cattle. "Steady, Loup, easy now!"

As Loup picked up speed, Amy crossed one rein over his neck and gave and took with the other to try to slow him.

Fallon was up ahead on her Arabian mare, Scout. She glanced over her shoulder as they approached and, as Amy and Loup went to pass them, she reached out and grabbed Loup's reins. Feeling the extra weight against him, Loup gave up his flight and returned to a walk alongside the Arabian.

"Thanks," Amy said in relief.

"Don't sweat it," Fallon told her. "It's not surprising he's spooking in here." She hesitated before speaking. "A word of advice. Loup's used to being up front. Sam was one of the senior wranglers. When the canyon opens up, take Loup farther forward. Trust him like you've asked him to trust you."

Amy stared after Fallon as the girl urged her horse forward. She was grateful for the suggestion, but did she have the courage to take it? "Do you want to go forward?" she murmured, leaning forward in the saddle.

Loup's ears flicked back at the sound of her voice.

"OK. I'll trust you, Loup." She patted his neck. "Just don't go running off like that again. You're not going to convince Hank to keep you at the ranch unless you settle down."

The canyon opened up into a vast expanse of prairie land dotted with cacti and trees. As the cattle and riders spread out, Amy shortened her reins. "OK, boy, let's see what you can do."

Loup plunged forward and for a moment she feared that she'd made the wrong decision in bringing him closer to the main action. But then the palomino opened into the most gorgeous gallop. It felt as if he could run forever and, as Amy's hair whipped back in the breeze, she tipped back her head and let out a whoop. She saw a gap that wasn't occupied by any of the wranglers where some of the cattle were starting to fall back from the main herd, so she pushed Loup forward and felt a thrill as the cows picked up their speed to rejoin the other cattle.

"Keep back!" Mike's voice cut into her exhilaration.

"I don't want him freaking out and causing an accident with the cattle."

"But — " Amy protested.

"Now!" Mike snapped before urging his buckskin after a cow and its calf that were straying away from the main herd.

Amy knew she had to respect his decision as one of the senior wranglers. "Come on, Loup," she sighed, pulling back on the reins. But Loup resisted her. "Loup!" Amy said more firmly. "Come on, we have to go back."

But the palomino pulled stubbornly in the same direction in which Mike had ridden. Amy wondered why the gelding should suddenly be ignoring her leg and hand prompts. "Come on, Loup. Partners, remember?" She put more pressure on her right rein and left leg. She glanced over at Mike to see if he had noticed the way Loup was suddenly fighting her. But Mike was in some trouble of his own and now Amy understood why Loup was defying her.

Mike had tried herding the cow and its calf back to the main group, but it was running blindly toward a ravine. Mike uncoiled his lasso and twirled it above his head before he sent it flying through the air with a neat flick of his wrist.

"Oh, no!" Amy gasped.

The cow, trying to protect its calf, suddenly switched direction and charged at Mike before he had a chance to secure the rope to his saddle horn. Instead of fighting Loup, Amy gave him his head, and the gelding hurtled toward Mike.

Mike's horse swerved and stumbled, almost falling to its knees. Mike was thrown clear and Amy watched in horror as the cow lowered its head and charged at the wrangler.

"Faster, Loup," she urged.

Gone was the frightened suspicious horse who had shied away from being ridden for so long. Loup was riding to Mike's rescue with a spirit as bold as any mountain lion. Amy could hear shouts and horse hooves drumming behind but she kept her focus on the frightened cow trying to protect her calf.

Amy's stomach twisted — it looked certain that the cow and Mike were going to collide. But Loup knew exactly what he was doing. With one incredible turn on his haunches, he cut straight across the cow's path, forcing it to swerve away from Mike.

Another figure raced past and reached for the cow's trailing rope, tying it around his saddle horn. *Will.*

Seconds later, Fallon galloped up on Scout. "Good job, Will! I'll take them back to the herd," she called. She unhitched the lasso and skillfully began to drive the cow and calf in the opposite direction.

Mike had already remounted his buckskin. Amy

thought he was going to ride by without a word, but the wrangler met her eyes. "I guess you've earned your place to ride up front," he told her gruffly, pulling his Stetson farther down on his head.

Amy held his gaze for a moment and then smiled at him. "I guess so," she said.

They broke for lunch a while later in a lush valley. Amy refilled the water container that hung on her saddle and ate her portion of sausages and beans, then went over to the horse line where Loup was hitched up and standing quietly. "You're doing great," she told him, giving him a cookie. Loup rubbed his head against her arm.

"Let's ride out!" Hank's voice carried through the air. The wranglers in the Jeeps were left to pack up camp while the rest of the ranch hands came for the horses.

Amy tightened Loup's girth and led him to a quieter space to mount. She was just rechecking her girth when one of the cattle dogs ran under Loup's legs.

Loup half reared and let out a whinny of fear. However brave he had been on the first part of the drive, the memory of the mountain lion attack hadn't left him. Amy knew she had to remind him of their bond and that she wasn't going to bail out and abandon him. She leaned forward and spoke in his ear, holding his reins in one hand and massaging his neck with the other. "I'm with you, Loup. I'm not going anywhere."

Loup stood stiff-legged and breathing hard, but he didn't rear up again. "Good boy," Amy said, keeping her fingers working on his neck.

"Go on, get!" Fallon yelled at the dog as she rode up on Scout. "You ready to go?"

Amy nodded.

"Maybe you can tell me something about your work," Fallon said as they rode side by side out of the valley. "I would have sworn that nothing was going to turn Loup around. I'd sure like to learn about whatever you did."

Amy smiled. "No problem."

Will rode up to join them and they took turns describing how they'd helped Loup with his recovery. As they were talking, the valley opened onto a lake toward which the cattle turned to drink.

They halted the horses and watched the sun dancing on the water's surface. Willow and ash trees fringed the far edge and beyond those, in the distance, were the magnificent mountains that were the one constant of the scenery they'd ridden through that day. Amy vowed that one day she'd come back for a longer visit.

The sun was low in the sky when they finally reached the summer pasture. Amy watched the cattle drop their heads to graze as soon as they realized they weren't being chased anymore. They'd remain here until the fall when they would be rounded up again and brought back to the ranch.

Amy felt a sense of sadness that she wouldn't be there to help with the return journey.

"Unless someone gives me a pillow to strap to my saddle, I'm not riding back tomorrow," Scooby groaned as he lowered himself onto the log beside Amy. They were all sitting around the campfire. Amy and Will glanced at each other.

"I don't know what you're complaining about, Scoob," Corey told him. "All you did was lope along at the back, taking photos."

"Yeah, I got a great one of you trying to rope a steer and hitting one of the ranch dogs instead." Scooby grinned.

When they climbed into their sleeping bags for a night under the bright starlit sky, Will propped himself up on his elbow to talk to Amy.

"All joking aside, you were great today. The way you cut that cow's flight was just awesome," he said quietly.

"It was more Loup than me," Amy said. "He knew exactly what to do. I've never ridden a horse that is so clearly thinking of every move ahead. I can see why he'd be unbeatable as a ranch horse with an experienced wrangler."

"Well, thanks to you, I don't think his future's in doubt anymore," Will said. "You're amazing, do you know that?"

Amy met his intense gaze. "You did great, too, grabbing the cow's rope like you were something out of a wild west rodeo show."

Usually, Will would have come back with a quip, but now when he spoke his voice was filled with earnestness. "We make a good team, don't we?"

We do. Amy knew it was true but she couldn't say the words out loud. She couldn't give Will hope that there could be anything but friendship between them.

She was painfully aware of Will's handsome profile against the night sky with the firelight playing over his features. He bent closer. "Amy . . ."

"Will, when I leave here, I'm going home. To Ty."

Will immediately pulled back. "Right. I'm sorry." His voice was taut with disappointment.

Amy reached for his arm and gave it a quick squeeze. Will had come to mean more to her over the last few days than she ever could have imagined. "You and I will always be great friends. Always."

But as she stared up at the crescent moon she knew that you could mean *always* with all your heart but there was still no guarantee of forever. She had thought she'd always stay at Heartland and yet that hadn't happened. She had thought her relationship with Ty would always survive no matter what, but now she wasn't so sure. She had thought she'd always feel and stay the same and yet she knew that her time away at school had changed her. *And so has being in Arizona.*

She felt a poignant sense of sadness. The future she'd had mapped out for as long as she could remember was changing, and she didn't know how to handle it.

Chapter Fourteen

When Amy saddled and mounted Loup the next day, there was a subtle difference in the gelding. While she knew he would never forget the savage attack, it was as if he was settled back into life as a cow pony. His head was high as he scented the air, his eyes alight with the enjoyment of belonging to the cattle drive.

"The boy is back." Hal grinned and gave Amy a high five as he passed her on his horse.

Amy felt so proud of the palomino as they made their way home. There was only one thing that soured the mood slightly, and that was the fact that Will wasn't riding alongside them. He rode the whole way with Max and, while Amy understood that her friend might be feeling awkward after the previous night, she wished that he felt he could still hang out with her.

Instead, she spent most of the ride either with Leila and Kirsten or Fallon. Fallon was still expressing a lot of interest in Amy's work and finally Amy put a proposition to her.

"Loup's going to need to carry on with his confidence-building or else he could slip back into focusing on his fear of the attack," she told Fallon. "If I showed you how to do T-touch and left you with some remedies, could you find some time to spend with him each day?"

Fallon didn't answer immediately and Amy thought for a moment that she was going to turn her down.

"I don't mind giving it a try," Fallon said at last, "but you're forgetting that Hank's still got to give Loup the thumbs-up to stay on the ranch."

Amy was stunned. "He wouldn't put Loup down after the way he behaved on the drive?"

"No," Fallon agreed, "but Mike's got such a problem with Loup that Hank might end up selling him. Don't forget, he did hurt Sam pretty bad."

Amy played the words again and again in her mind, but she couldn't see any way out for Loup if Mike decided to put pressure on Hank to sell him. It was so unfair.

• They didn't reach Shallow Creek until late in the evening. Amy rubbed Loup down and gave him his feed before preparing him an extra-deep bed. "You did so well. I'm proud of you," she told the quarterhorse who gave a long snort into his bucket. "I'll come see you in the morning." Just saying the words triggered her anxiety. Loup belonged at Shallow Creek Ranch. It would be a poor reward for all of his years' service if he ended up being sent elsewhere without someone to carry on with helping him heal.

℮

When Amy woke on Monday morning, she swung her legs off her bed and groaned. It wasn't just the long hours in the saddle that had made her ache, but the previous night on the hard ground under the stars had made matters worse. She dreaded to think what it would have been like without Grandpa's padded bedroll. The other ranch hands made similar noises of protest as they got washed and dressed at half their previous speed.

All Amy could manage to eat at breakfast was an apple. She decided to go down to the yard to give Loup an extra-thorough grooming so he would look his best.

When she opened the door to his stall, she found Will had beaten her to it. "Great minds think alike, huh?" he greeted her.

Amy smiled back and took a body brush out of the grooming kit. "Absolutely."

They worked in silence, but the awkwardness that had been between them the day before was gone.

When they heard deep male voices just outside, Amy

glanced at Will. "It'll be fine," he said reassuringly. "Loup's earned his place here."

Amy nodded. She couldn't bring herself to share with him what Fallon had told her.

"Here goes," she said, and took a deep breath before leaving Loup's stall. Will followed her and Amy was pleased to see Loup immediately look out over the door to check where they were going.

"Mike was just telling me how you and Loup saved him from being trampled by a cow," Hank said without preamble. "Good work."

Amy wondered if surprise showed on her face as she looked at Mike.

The wrangler shrugged. "That still doesn't change the fact that I don't want him here."

Amy appealed to Hank. "You said Loup was the best horse on this ranch and you hoped I'd succeed. Well, Will and I have, you can't argue with that. Loup deserves a chance."

"He's not being put down, that's for sure," Hank agreed. "But I'm afraid I just can't keep him on the ranch."

Amy's shoulders slumped and she stared at Loup's noble face in despair. He didn't deserve this. He should be at home with someone who would continue to work with him.

"Loup stays," a voice called out firmly from behind them.

Amy turned along with the others to see a sandy-haired man propelling himself in a wheelchair across the yard.

Hank was the first to react. "Hey, Sam, it's good to see you." He stepped forward to shake his hand. "I was glad to hear you aren't quite as bad off as we thought." There was a strong likeness between the man in the wheelchair and Mike, making it obvious that this was his brother, the ranch hand who had ridden Loup the longest.

Sam wheeled himself up close to Loup's stall. "It's good to see you, too, Hank, and this fella."

Amy held her breath as Loup scented Sam. Would he reject his old partner because of the mountain lion attack?

Loup gave a low wicker and nuzzled Sam's outstretched hand. Amy realized she shouldn't have doubted him for a moment. *Horses are so much more forgiving than people.* Loup had allowed the bond between himself and a rider to be reestablished, but Amy felt like he had one final step to take. He needed to know that Sam didn't bear him a grudge over his fall. Loup was such an honest horse, the knowledge that he had in turn let his partner down might end up setting back his recovery. Amy felt that the path was now clear for Loup to put the past behind him once and for all.

"Fallon called me and brought me up to speed with

what's been going on." Sam looked at Will and Amy. "I guess I have you two to thank for undoing the damage that I did."

"Are you nuts?" Mike burst out. "Damage that *you* did? Loup almost broke your back!"

"I was the one who made the mistake in that canyon," Sam said passionately. "I don't blame him for freaking out when I tried getting on him a second time. And he wasn't trying to injure me, he just didn't want me taking him back out into danger."

Amy felt a real warmth toward Sam. He truly understood Loup. "I think Loup might have struggled at some point with the fact that he'd hurt you. But by coming here today, you're setting him free from those feelings of guilt."

"It's only what he deserves, and I guess I'm being a little selfish since I'd like to think that my old partner will be waiting here for me when I come back." Sam looked at Hank, who nodded.

"If that's what you want, then your saddle's ready for you as soon as you're back on your feet," he promised.

Mike held up his hands in the air. "I give up. Sam, you're as loopy as your horse. The only thing right about him is his name."

Suddenly, they were all chuckling. Amy placed her arms around Loup's neck. "You did it. You're safe!"

❧

On Tuesday morning, Amy went down to breakfast for the last time on the ranch. She was flying back to Heartland in a couple of hours to enjoy the last day or so before she went back to school.

Amy took her tray over to where she saw Max sitting and, after a few minutes, Will joined them, too.

"I'm going to miss ranch-style breakfasts when we get back," he said, adding some ketchup to a plate loaded with bacon, egg, beans, sausages, and toast.

Amy grinned. "If you tried eating all of that in college you wouldn't get to your morning lectures until they were halfway through."

"It would be worth it," Will told her. "And the way I see it, I burned up enough energy over the last two days. I earned this."

"Ditto," Max agreed. "I'm off for seconds."

"So," Will said, "are you all packed?" He was driving her to the airport to catch her flight, and Amy had arranged for Soraya to pick her up when she arrived.

"Yeah," Amy said. "All I have left to do now is go say good-bye to Loup."

"And Fallon's going to take over his care until Sam comes back?"

Amy nodded. "Would you believe that she's challenged Mike to a barrel race with her riding Loup?"

"Nothing that girl does surprises me," Will admitted. "She's one of a kind."

Max sat back down with them. "We'll have to swap e-mail addresses before you go. I'm predicting a reunion for next year's cattle drive."

Amy and Will's eyes met. This had been such an amazing experience, only the thought of returning someday made leaving bearable.

"It would be great to come back," Amy agreed.

Loup was turned out in one of the smaller paddocks. Amy and Will climbed onto the gate and just watched him for a while. The quarterhorse was standing nose-to-tail with Scout. When Amy and Will's scent carried down to the gelding on the breeze, Loup raised his head and sniffed the air. He stared at them and then crossed the paddock in a beautiful fluid trot. Amy reached out and gripped Will's arm. She couldn't quite believe that this was the last time they'd see him.

"Hey, fella," Will greeted Loup when the palomino thrust his nose over the gate. "You're looking great."

Amy had to agree with Will. There was a vitality to the ranch horse that had been missing before the cattle drive. She reached out to scratch between the palomino's eyes. "I guess this is good-bye. Fallon's going to look after you now. You're going to be all right."

"He'd better be," Fallon said cheerfully as she joined them. "I'm going to be spending enough time with him." But the way she scratched Loup gently between his eyes belied her casual words.

Amy knew that it was going to be hard to leave the palomino, but knowing that he was in Fallon's care made it easier. Despite the ranch hand's tough exterior, Amy knew how much she was prepared to invest in Loup so that he would be ready for Sam when he came back.

She looked at Will and saw the same relief in his eyes. "He's going to be fine," Amy said.

Will ran his hand down the palomino's neck. "Thanks to you, he is."

Amy slipped her arms around Loup for one last time. "Take it easy, boy. You're home, where you belong."

Loup touched his nose to her shoulder and rested it there as if he knew that this was good-bye. Amy knew she should have been ready to let go, but suddenly it was one of the hardest things she had ever done. "Good-bye, Loup," she murmured. "I'll never forget you."

On the plane ride home, Amy tried to think through all that had happened in the last few days. *Loup is saved and I'm flying back to be where I belong — with Ty,* she told herself again and again. Everything was the way it should be. So why did she feel that something was missing?

She sighed and pressed her forehead against the window. *Going home doesn't make me feel complete anymore.* There. She'd admitted it.

Amy blinked back burning tears. Deep in her soul she knew she would always belong to Heartland, but right now she needed to explore every opportunity that life had to offer. She closed her eyes against a sharp pain. Right now, Amy needed more than Heartland could give her. She needed more than her mother's memory. More than her family. More than the horses. *More than Ty.*

Amy got off her flight feeling empty. A part of her wanted to run from the conclusion she'd reached on the plane. She wanted to go back to Heartland and keep pretending that everything was the same. But to be fair to Ty, and to be honest with herself, she knew that couldn't happen.

Soraya was waiting for her at the airport. Amy forced a cheerful smile for her friend. Anthony had come along for the ride so Soraya could introduce him to Amy before they all headed back to school. He was sitting in the front seat, waiting for the girls to return, but he jumped out to help Amy with her things as soon as the two of them came into view.

"Hey, Amy!" Anthony said cheerfully as he reached for her luggage. "It's great to finally meet you. Soraya has told me so much about you. I don't know how she's really surviving on her own at school, considering how much she talks about your friendship."

Amy gave Anthony a quick hug. "It's great to meet you, too. I've heard great things about you." Amy paused. "I hope you'll forgive me, but I'm feeling pretty wiped out. It's been a long couple of days."

"Don't give it a second thought," Anthony said reassuringly. "I totally understand. Why don't you make yourself comfortable and just relax until we get you home?"

Amy gave Anthony a grateful look. He seemed like a good guy and she was sorry she didn't have the energy to get to know him a little bit during the car ride. But right now, she just needed some time to prepare herself for what she knew was coming when she got home.

Climbing into the backseat, Amy settled herself in and put on her sunglasses. It was a beautiful spring day, but the cheerfulness of the weather couldn't penetrate the sadness that was overwhelming her heart.

"So, how was it?" Soraya asked once they were on their way. "Do you feel like a real cowgirl?"

Amy took a deep breath to steady herself before replying. "It was great," she replied with a reluctant smile. But that was all she could bring herself to say. She would have liked the chance to talk things through with Soraya before arriving at home, but she didn't feel like she could do that with Anthony in the car. Amy didn't want his first impression of her to be colored by her current emotions.

"I bet you've missed Ty," Soraya commented as they drove along the country lane toward Heartland. "It must have been so tough leaving him after how psyched you were about spending your spring break together."

Amy was glad she had her sunglasses on so that Soraya and Anthony couldn't see the tears in her eyes. She twisted her Claddagh ring and thought about what a different person she was from the one who had received the ring all those months ago. Back then, her hopes, dreams, and aspirations had been wrapped up in Ty. Now, she couldn't see the future exactly, but she knew it didn't rest in him.

Amy closed her eyes against the burning tears. How could she ever bring herself to say those words to Ty?

Soraya dropped her off outside the farmhouse; Amy knew she was expecting to be invited inside so Amy could spend some time with Anthony but she needed to speak with Ty too urgently to wait.

"Thanks so much for the ride. I'll call you later," she promised as she lifted her luggage out of the back of her friend's car. "It was really great to meet you, Anthony. Next time I hope we can talk a little more," Amy added apologetically. "I'm not always this out of it."

"Don't worry about it," Anthony said. "We'll have lots of chances to get to know each other, I'm sure."

Soraya looked a little surprised and disappointed but she lowered the window and waved as she drove off. "I'll talk to you soon," she called to Amy. Maybe Soraya had even guessed what was going through Amy's head — they were such old friends that they could often tell what the other was thinking even if it wasn't spoken out loud.

Amy dropped her bag inside the back door and made her way down to the barn where Ty was getting the evening feeds ready.

"Amy!" Ty put down the buckets he was carrying. He pushed his dark hair off his forehead in an agonizingly familiar gesture. As he reached out his arms to sweep her up into a close embrace, Amy took a step back.

"Ty . . . I . . . I missed you . . . but we need to talk."

Amy felt as if a cold vice had clamped around her heart at the instant confusion that appeared in Ty's eyes.

"Is everything OK? Are you OK?"

"Yes . . . no." To her horror, Amy felt the tears she'd managed to control in the car flood into her eyes. She took a deep breath. "I don't know the right way to say this, so I'm going to ask you to forgive me if I say the wrong thing."

Ty didn't break his steady gaze. "Did I do something wrong?"

"No!" The response tore out of Amy. "Never."

Jasmine, the black dressage pony who had been at

Heartland for as long as Sundance, put her head over her stall and whickered gently.

Amy wanted nothing more than to go and put her arms around her, but she knew she had to deal with her decision and face Ty.

"Ty . . ." Her voice broke. *You have to do this. It's only fair. To you. To Ty.*

She took another deep breath. "I've had time to think when I was away and . . ." *This is the hardest thing I've ever had to do.* ". . . and I can't get it out of my head that we need to take a step back from each other. We both have so much ahead of us, and right now, the time isn't right for us to face it together." Her breath came in shudders. "I love you, Ty. But it just doesn't feel the way it used to. Maybe sometime in the future . . . but not now. Not for either of us."

Before she could say anything else, Ty pulled her close. She could feel his chest wracked with the same uneven breathing as her own. He held her for a moment before speaking. "I know." His own voice sounded close to breaking. "I think we've both been coming to this for a while. You're just braver than I am in being able to say it."

"You felt it, too?" Amy whispered. *Why am I surprised? We've always seen things the same way, even as our relationship has changed.* Amy considered this for a moment. *I guess that even though some things between us are ending, there are other ways that we're connected that will always be there for us.* She hurt in a way she'd never felt before, but the realization that she and Ty would continue to share a connection eased that pain just a little.

For a moment that felt like an eternity, they clung to each other before Amy stepped back. She looked down at the Claddagh ring that Ty had given her while at the same time promising to love her forever.

"Keep it." Ty covered her hand with his own. "Our friendship will never end, and you should know that I'll always be here for you."

Amy made herself meet his gaze and saw her own pain reflected in the green depths of his eyes. "Thank you, Ty," she whispered before the tears spilled down her cheeks.

Amy knew that Heartland and her family would always be there for her, and now she felt that Ty, though in a different way than before, would always be there for her, too. When she left home this time, she'd be going back to school with a new perspective — no longer would Amy be constantly looking back to Heartland; now was the time to start looking forward to find out what lay beyond the horizon.